More than forty years before the disappearance of three Montgomery College students, the woods of Burkittsville, Maryland, were home to another ghastly tragedy. Seven children were murdered at the hands of a hermit named Rustin Parr. With his admission of guilt, and subsequent execution, his official confession was accepted as truth. But did he kill the Burkittsville Seven?

BLAIR WITCH
The Secret Confession of Rustin Parr

On November 22, 1941, a hermit named Rustin Parr swung from the gallows at Rockville State Penitentiary, put to death for the murder of seven innocent young children. Was Parr the crazed killer the state of Maryland made him out to be—or an innocent man, caught in the grip of forces beyond his ken or control?

Perhaps the only man who can answer those questions is Dominick Cazale, the priest who heard Parr's jailhouse confession. For sixty years, Cazale kept his vow to Parr—and God—and remained silent about the words that passed between the two men. But now, tortured by a terrible secret of his own, Cazale is finally ready to lay bare the truth about Rustin Parr's last, desperate days . . . and the evil that haunts the woods of the Black Hills.

This book is a work of fiction. Names, characters, places and incidents are products of the author's imagination or are used fictitiously. Any resemblance to actual events or locales or persons living or dead is entirely coincidental.

An *Original* Publication of POCKET BOOKS

POCKET BOOKS, a division of Simon and Schuster, Inc.
1230 Avenue of the Americas, New York, NY 10020

Copyright © 2000 Artisan Pictures Inc.

The epigraph on page v is taken from *Satanism and Witchcraft* by Jules Michelet. Copyright © 1939 by Citadel Press. All rights reserved.

ISBN: 0-7434-1153-6

First Pocket Books trade paperback printing August 2000

10 9 8 7 6 5 4 3 2 1

POCKET and colophon are registered trademarks of Simon & Schuster, Inc.

Printed in the U.S.A.

The Sorceress . . . appears none knows from whence, a monster, an aerolite from the skies. Who so bold, great God! as to come nigh her? Where is her lurking-place? In untracked wilds, in impenetrable forests of bramble, on blasted heaths, where entangled thistles suffer no foot to pass. She must be sought by night, cowering beneath some old-world dolmen. If you find her, she is isolated still by the common horror of the countryside; she has, as it were, a ring of fire round her haunts.

—Jules Michelet
Satanism and Witchcraft

BLAIR WITCH

The
Secret Confession
of
Rustin Parr

chapter one

Hospitals reek of death.

Oh, they try to disguise it—place a vase of sweet-smelling flowers in the reception area, hang photographs on the walls of gap-toothed, smiling children hugging their doctors, pipe in the bouncy, effervescent sounds of Muzak for you to hum along with while you wait—but spend any time in a hospital at all, and you'll soon come to recognize those things for what they really are.

Camouflage.

Anesthesia.

Distractions.

In the seventeen years since I'd last been there, Broward County General had greatly improved the quality of its distractions.

The institutional white I remembered was out; peach—the color of the carpet in the reception area, and the wall, starting at the waist-high wooden railing and continuing on up to the ceiling—was in. The slate-blue cushioned chairs and couches in the new reception area would have looked right at home in any corporate office. The main entrance had been entirely rebuilt: it was now covered by a soaring vault of glass windows. Paintings and photographs (landscapes mostly) hung all along a long, high-ceilinged corridor that led from automatic, sliding glass doors to the front desk.

Heading down that corridor toward the main desk, I passed two like Broward since I could remember. His health had never been good: an infantryman in World War I, he'd lost his hearing in the trenches and gotten a bad back in the bargain. Not that he ever talked about that pain: that was his own particular cross to bear. The way of the world, at least as he knew it. A man's feelings were his own, a woman's place was in the kitchen, children should be seen and not heard. Men wore hats, went to church on Sunday (or in my grandfather's case, temple on Saturday), and stayed loyal to company, country, and wife their whole life long. To do otherwise was unthinkable.

When he got sick and went into Broward, I was in Florida, doing research for a novelist up in St. Augustine. During the week, I'd be working, but when Friday came, I'd drive down the coast and stay with my grandmother. The two of us would visit my grandfather in the hospital and have dinner. The usual topic of conversation: how the world had changed since they were young. Changed, in my grandfather's opinion, not for the better.

Which, coincidentally enough, was exactly what Dominick Cazale and I had spent an afternoon discussing the first time we'd met face-to-face.

Cazale, though, had an entirely different take on things.

"Listen to them," Cazale had said. He was talking about two twenty-something men in black turtlenecks sitting behind us at the bar, who were arguing about investment strategies. One of them had just used the word *crash* in the same sentence with *stock market*.

"They have no idea." Cazale shook his head. "They're wondering which SUV to buy. Back then, we wondered how many meals you could make out of a can of beans."

It was Thanksgiving weekend, 1999; we were squeezed into a little booth in the back room of the Corner Bistro, corner of Twelfth and Jane in New York City. When Cazale had told me to pick a place to meet, I had immediately thought of this one. It had character, one of the few authentic New York spots left in the gaudy tourist attraction Manhattan had become. Dim lights, dark wood booths, darker wood tables, covered with years of graffiti and grease. And the best hamburger in the city, thick enough you had to use two hands to hold it, and even then you weren't guaranteed of getting your mouth all the way around. Especially if you ordered the Bistro Burger, which added three strips of bacon, slices of raw onion, and another quarter inch to the burger's height.

Dominick and I both had Bistro Burgers and black and tans in front of us. "This much meat, it would have fed all four of us—me, my mother, and my brothers. In fact, if we'd been able to afford this, my ma would probably have invited the neighbors over to share . . ." His voice trailed off. "Well. You don't want to hear my sob stories. Let's just say people should count themselves lucky to be alive in this day and age."

He'd raised his voice on the word *lucky*. One of the men at the bar (who had, I saw, pulled out a cell phone and was talking on it) glanced back and glared at us.

Cazale was a big man, with intense blue eyes, a craggy, lined face, and a habit of using his hands when he spoke—clenching them into fists, punching the air, hitting the table. The longer he talked, in fact, the more he reminded me of an ex-prizefighter. Given the colorful life he'd led, I wouldn't have been surprised if he had stepped into the ring a time or two.

It was nice to finally put a face to the voice. We'd spoken on the phone several times while I was preparing *The Blair Witch Project Dossier* for publication. During one of those calls, we discovered we'd both be in New York City for Thanksgiving, and arranged to have lunch.

We discovered we had quite a few things in common, chief among them, a passion for history. It was my work; it had been Cazale's life. He'd spent thirty years teaching it, first in New York City and then California, working well past the point his union contract had called for him to retire.

He taught mostly junior high school, because "I like them when they're smart enough to get my jokes, and too young to know how corny they are."

As we talked that afternoon, though, what came across to me was that he liked students at that age because he could really reach them: he could make a difference in their lives. And making a difference was what Dominick Cazale's own life had been all about. Not just as a teacher: he'd volunteered for the Peace Corps; in the sixties, he'd been active in the civil rights movement. He'd marched with Chavez, built houses with Jimmy Carter for Habitat for Humanity.

Though they couldn't have been more different physically, Cazale reminded me of Carter in at least one way: he had the same conviction in man's Christian duty—in the best sense of the word—that the former president did.

I learned a little bit about every part of Dominick Cazale's life that afternoon: his youth, his military service, his years as a history teacher, and a particularly painful series of summers he'd spent as an assistant Little League coach, trying to teach his charges the importance of putting the bat on the ball.

We even touched lightly on those years he spent as a priest, serving the Roman Catholic community in Frederick County, Maryland.

But the awful thing that happened in 1941, the thing that had brought us together in the first place . . .

That, we never talked about at all.

Judge Kara slammed down her gavel, and that show ended. A soap opera began.

Gert and her friend left.

The woman in the chair next to me shifted position; the little boy came and sat on her lap.

"Excuse me."

I looked up.

A man dressed in a white lab coat—thirty-five, Hispanic, with thick black hair and a day's worth of stubble—was standing over me.

"I'm Dr. Juarez. Pete Juarez."

I stood and introduced myself.

"Thanks for coming."

"I wish I'd known earlier," I said. "How is he?"

"Like I said on the phone "—Juarez sat down on the couch next to me—"we're astonished he's still alive." He yawned. "Sorry. Late night." He yawned again. "Dominick had third-degree burns on close to thirty percent of his body. Normally, in cases like this, the rule of thumb is to add the patient's age to the percent of the body that was severely burned. If you get a count of more than a hundred . . . well, you don't expect them to live. Especially when you're dealing with older patients."

"So you think he'll be all right?"

"Some good signs today. He seems to be coming out of his coma now . . . though he's still got a long way to go." Juarez smiled. "But at this point . . . yes, I think he'll pull through."

"Can I see him?"

Juarez looked at his watch. "The nurse is changing his dressings now. Why don't I come back and get you in forty-five minutes or so?"

"Sure." I yawned myself then. "Sorry. Long flight."

"You want some coffee? The cafeteria's just down the hall."

"Actually, that sounds great," I said.

"I could use one too. I'll show you the way."

He led. I followed.

"Dominick taught my tenth-grade American history class. Two teachers quit at the same time, and he came out of retirement to do the principal a favor. I used to think he was such a hard-ass." Juarez smiled. "Now . . . I don't know where I'd be without him. Not here, that's for sure."

The hallway we were walking through had been another victim of the hospital's makeover: yellows and brighter whites here. More landscapes, more smiling children.

"Sounds like he made an impression on you."

"Oh, yeah. He gave me this one assignment; I'll never forget it. He wrote a list of like thirty names on the blackboard—Washington, Benjamin Franklin, Thomas Jefferson, guys like that—and everyone in the class had to pick the one they thought was the most important person in the Revolutionary War and do a report on them."

Two nurses in pink scrubs walked by and nodded hello. Juarez nodded back.

"The thing was, nobody in the class could pick the same person. So I was in the back row, and by the time it was my turn to pick, every name I knew was gone. So you know who I got?"

I shook my head. "Who?"

"Lafayette."

"Ah." I smiled.

"You know Lafayette?"

"A little. But then—history is pretty much what I do for a living."

"You're a teacher?"

"No, I do mostly research. A little writing."

"So that's how you and Dominick met?"

"More or less."

Juarez nodded. "He's going to have a hard time without Mary. A really hard time. They were so close."

"I never knew her."

"A sweet, sweet woman." Juarez shook his head. "The way she died—it's horrible. Just horrible." Ahead of us were a set of wooden double doors. "Here's the cafeteria."

"So he's coming out of the coma?"

"Seems to be. Has the classic indicators. Brain activity is up; we're seeing some involuntary muscle movement . . . the nurse who checked on him last night heard him talking to himself. That's a real good sign."

I was curious. "What was he saying?"

"Nothing that made sense, but that's okay. The significant thing is that he is talking at all." Juarez reached the cafeteria door and held it open for me. "He was going on about something that rusted, according to the nurse. 'Rusted, forgive me.' "

The door almost hit me as I walked through. "What?"

"Something that rusted," Juarez repeated. " 'It rusted, I'm sorry. Rusted, I apologize.' " He looked at me. "That mean something to you?"

I looked at him, and past, into the large, sunlit cafeteria we'd just entered.

It was lunchtime: the room was full of people eating, talking, and laughing. Wall-length windows covered the right side of the cafeteria; through them, a perfect Florida day was visible, eighty-five degrees, blue sky, not a cloud visible for miles.

Palm trees swayed lazily back and forth, a sprinkler sprayed water in neat lines across an immaculately trimmed row of hedges.

It was easy to imagine children running through that sprinkler, tumbling on the lawn, laughing and playing. Hide-and-seek, freeze tag, duck-duck-goose.

I saw children now, in my mind's eye. Eight of them.

Four girls, four boys.

They walked where there was no sun, through a pitch-dark forest, to the steps of a run-down, ramshackle old house, its front porch overgrown with weeds. A figure stood in the open doorway, half-hidden by shadows, waiting.

"Are you all right?" Juarez was staring at me.

"Yeah." The sunlit cafeteria suddenly seemed unnaturally bright. "Just thinking about something."

Thinking, in fact, about the figure in the doorway. The hermit in the forest who killed seven of the eight little children before turning himself in.

His name was Rustin Parr.

"So does that mean anything to you, what Cazale said?" the doctor asked. " 'Rusted, I'm sorry'?"

I looked straight into Juarez's eyes.

The night before Parr was executed for his crimes, a young priest had heard his confession. It all happened sixty years ago, in the town of Burkittsville, Maryland.

The young priest was Dominick Cazale.

"No," I lied. "It doesn't mean a thing to me."

"I'll get the coffees. You grab a seat, okay? There." Juarez pointed to a long, crowded table toward the back of the room.

I nodded and made my way across the cafeteria.

chapter two

In 1785—some four years after Lafayette had saved
the American Revolution at Yorktown—a woman named Elly
Kedward was bound to a wheelbarrow and escorted from the village
of Blair, Maryland. Accused of drawing blood from the town's children for the purposes of practicing witchcraft, Kedward was tied to a
tree in the forests surrounding Blair and left to the mercy of the ele-
ments. It was the dead of winter. Presumably, she died of exposure.

The following summer, the town's children began disappearing
en masse.

Terrified parents were convinced it was Kedward come back to
take her revenge. They abandoned their "cursed" village, which—
shortly thereafter—ceased to exist.

There begins the legend of the Blair Witch.

This is long past the time of the Salem witch trials, and even further removed from the days of the great European witch-hunts: Elly
Kedward's execution is a historical incongruity. It is incongruous in
other ways as well, because after 1824, the curse becomes as much
tied to Kedward as it does to the place where she was abandoned: the
aptly named Black Hills of Maryland.

In 1824, a Baltimore land baron named Peter Burkitt founds
Burkittsville on the spot where Blair once stood. His town incorpo-
rates portions of the Black Hills.

Burkittsville is quickly settled, mostly by German immigrants—names such as Lenhardt, Moeller, and Bauch dominate the town tax rolls.

Most of these immigrants are farmers: they grow wheat, corn, and rye; they raise sheep, cattle, and pigs. Simple, hardworking folk, by and large Lutherans, not given to superstition.

But what happens next in their town gives them reason to pause and consider.

In 1825, another young child—eleven-year-old Eileen Treacle—drowns in nearby Tappy East Creek. Witnesses testify to seeing an old woman's hand reach out and pull the girl under the water. Her body is never found.

In 1886, it's an eight-year-old girl named Robin Weaver who disappears. She turns up a few days later, safe and sound. However, a five-man search party sent after her vanishes, according to some reports, disemboweled. The bodies of the searchers are never found.

And in 1941 . . .

Rustin Parr.

The other people at the table were all doctors; Juarez introduced me as a friend of Cazale's.

"You've got good timing," one of them said to me. "It looks like your friend's coming out of it."

I nodded. "That's what I hear."

"Poor guy." There were nods of assent around the table. "He's not going to have an easy time of it."

"Have you had any luck tracking down his charts, Pete?" another doctor said to Juarez. "Anything that would explain—"

"No," Juarez said abruptly.

"Because you know that detective is going to be all over you."

"Yeah, he was here again," another said. "Did you see him?"

"No," Juarez said. "No, I didn't. Can we talk about something else, please?"

The group fell silent.

Juarez drummed his fingers on the table, then stood up. "I think I'll get something to eat. Anybody else?"

Heads shook. Juarez pushed his chair away from the table and walked back to the end of the line. The other doctors offered smiles acknowledging my presence, then slowly returned to talking among themselves.

I sipped at my coffee.

The police? What did they have to do with all this?

It took Juarez ten minutes to return. By the time he sat down again, all the other doctors had left.

Whatever was bothering Juarez, he clearly didn't want to talk about it. And his colleagues were willing to give him that space. I decided to respect that space too . . . for the moment.

"That other doctor said Cazale wouldn't have an easy time of it," I prompted.

"Yeah. Recovering from this will be a long, painful process." Juarez had come back with a chocolate doughnut. He took a bite of it now. "I don't know how much you know about burn victims—"

"Not much."

"Well . . . you know what third-degree burns are?"

"They're the worst ones, right? First degree, second degree, then third."

"That's right. Dominick had extensive third-degree burns, over most of the right side of his body. Down to the muscle, in some spots. The skin won't grow back. So, we have to replace it."

"From other parts of his body?" I had heard of those kinds of procedures.

Juarez nodded. "We're lucky, in that there were large portions of undamaged skin we can use—the backs of his legs, his buttocks. There was a guy in Milwaukee—famous case—who was so badly burned that the only undamaged skin was on the bottoms of his feet. They had to harvest it, sheet by sheet. Cut it off, sew it on, let more grow, and repeat. On the bottoms of his feet. Can you imagine how painful that must have been?" Juarez shook his head. "Jesus."

Despite myself, I shuddered. "So when do you start that procedure?"

"Oh, we started it already. Better to do it now, while he can't really feel it."

"Sure," I said, hoping that was true.

We both fell silent for a moment.

"He's a tough guy, Dominick," Juarez said. "A real fighter. I think he'll pull through just fine."

I nodded. "Do you think he knows about his wife?"

"Well, that seems to be the question of the day . . . of the week, really. It's what Detective Yamana wants to talk to him about."

"He's the detective the other doctor mentioned?"

Juarez nodded. "This guy—he's obsessed."

"About?"

"He says there's something suspicious about how the fire started. It's crazy. These things happen all the time. A lit match, a frayed electrical cord, who knows." Juarez took a sip of his coffee, then grimaced. "Christ. I keep forgetting how bad this coffee is. There's a Dunkin' Donuts around the corner—we should've gone there."

"That's all right," I said. "So the police?"

"Yeah." Juarez sighed. "They found evidence of an accelerant at the scene. Gasoline. They're calling it arson."

"Arson? That doesn't make any sense."

Juarez nodded.

"Who would do a thing like that?"

"Well." He picked the half-eaten doughnut up from his plate and broke it in two. "The cops think it was Cazale."

America was so busy watching the monsters overseas, it missed the one in its midst.

Rustin Parr should have waited for a slow news day: then his name might resonate today the way Jack the Ripper's does. In 1941, after all, serial killers didn't come along every few months the way they do these days: they were a rarity. And serial killers who kidnapped and killed small children . . .

You could hardly make up a better bogeyman.

But that year, the papers had bigger fish to fry. The world was falling apart, and by this time all but the most die-hard isolationists clearly saw that the United States was going to have to step in and put it back together. Things weren't going well at home, either: just a few years removed from the darkest days of the Depression, labor unions were at the height of their power and influence. Union men and union busters alike were being beaten and often killed. Union leaders were kingpins with power to rival that of elected politicians.

In the midst of those tumultuous times, Rustin Parr rated national headlines on only two occasions: the day he walked into W. W. Smith's General Store in Burkittsville and told the people there, "I'm finally finished," and the day he was hanged.

Burt Atkins, who owned the store, thought at first Parr was referring to the wagonload of dog food the hermit had bought on his last visit into town.

It wasn't until Sheriff Damon Bowers and his deputy hiked four hours into the Black Hills, to Parr's house, that they knew what he really meant.

Bowers and Deputy Hobart found the bodies of seven little children buried in Parr's basement. On their way back into town, they were accosted by the eighth child who had gone missing from Burkittsville during the seven months between November 1940 and May 1941.

From twelve-year-old Kyle Brody, they learned the horrible details of Parr's crimes: how he'd kidnapped the children . . . and what he'd done to them afterwards. Kyle provided explicit descriptions to the authorities, told them how Parr had forced him to march down to the basement with his victims, to stand in the corner, his back to Parr, and listen.

What he'd heard haunted Kyle Brody the rest of his life: he was in and out of mental institutions until the day he died.

Parr himself said nothing about the killings publicly. When he finally gave a news conference a few days before his execution, he made a number of cryptic comments, at times seeming to blame "voices in his head" for the crime. The local media pounced on this, turning his crimes into the latest manifestation of the Blair Witch legend, for surely Elly Kedward had been the one whispering in Rustin's ear while he wielded his knife.

No one would ever know for sure, however: Parr went to the gallows without uttering another word about the crimes. Any possible explanation for his actions, or the voices in his head, died with him.

Except for what he confessed to Father Dominick Cazale the night before his execution.

Cazale had never revealed to anyone what Parr had told him, had only insisted that he believed Rustin, like all of God's children, was a soul worthy of absolution . . . even salvation.

He never talked much about the matter at all, to me or to others. When we'd met in New York, the words *Rustin Parr* had never crossed Dominick's lips.

Though the last time we talked on the phone, six months or so after our Thanksgiving rendezvous . . . I'd had an inkling that Burkittsville wasn't far from his mind.

"Why?" I asked Juarez. "What possible reason could Cazale have for burning down his own house?"

"That's what the cop wants to know. This Detective Yamana."

Juarez's beeper went off.

"Excuse me a second." He pulled the pager out of his pocket and studied it.

"Talk about timing. Let's go."

"What is it?"

He stood up and clipped the beeper back on his belt. "Dominick's awake."

We left the cafeteria by a different door than when we'd entered and passed through a part of the hospital that was immediately familiar to me: the intensive care unit, where I'd spent so much time with my grandfather two decades earlier.

"Before we go in, I should warn you. He's going to look pretty bad."

I nodded.

"Do you want me to give you specifics, so you won't be surprised?"

I shook my head. "No, that's all right. I've seen some pretty gruesome scenes—"

"It's not your being able to take it I'm worried about," Juarez interrupted. "It's the effect your reaction will have on him."

"What should I do?"

"Be natural. Don't stare at him—but don't look away, either. Okay?"

"All right."

As we turned the next corner, a man pushed past us.

" 'Scuze me, Doc!"

"Toby, what's up?" Juarez called after him.

The man—Toby—didn't even bother turning around. "Your patient's freaking out, all right?"

Toby disappeared through a set of double glass doors ahead of us.

"Another patient?" I asked. "Listen, if you have to go, just point me in the direction of—"

Juarez started running too. "No!" he called over his shoulder. "He's talking about Cazale!"

Juarez pushed the glass doors open and went through.

I stood there a moment, unsure of what to do.

Then, in the absence of instructions, I started off after him.

chapter three

A *bronze plaque above the glass double doors* read
THE CHARLES AND PHOEBE CONANT BURN CENTER. I glanced
up at it as I passed through.

The hospital beyond was new construction—not another renovation, but a completely separate building: immaculate white corridors,
cool blue trim, gray carpeting. The corridor widened; I passed a long
counter to the right, a seating area to the left.

HOW CAN WE HELP? a sign behind the counter asked.

The reception area, but it was deserted now. I caught glimpses of
flat-panel computer screens, chairs pushed back from work areas, a
plate full of half-eaten food, before I was by the counter, and the corridor narrowed again.

A sign above my head said:

> AUTHORIZED PERSONNEL ONLY
> BEYOND THIS POINT

I ignored it.

Ahead of me, Juarez turned to his right and disappeared. I followed, hearing the sound of raised voices as I turned the corner.

And stopped.

Somehow, I'd walked onto the set of a science fiction movie.

At least that's how it seemed to me at first; the hallway had ended, depositing me in a room of glass and shining steel. Part of a spaceship: a control room of some sort. In the center of the room was an island, a long, narrow table with a half dozen flat-panel computer screens on it. Workstations.

One side of the room was the entrance to the hallway I'd just come from.

The other three sides were taken up by huge chrome doors, with glass viewing panels set in the center of each. Three doors to either side of me, two directly ahead. Hospital rooms, I realized, then noticed a soft blue light—ultraviolet light—coming through the panel to my immediate right. Then I understood: this entire area had been especially designed for severely burned patients, just like Dominick Cazale.

The light, the soundproof doors, and the ward's isolation: this was intended as a quiet, calm place—a place of healing.

Right now, though, it was a madhouse.

The door to one of the rooms in front of me had been slid to one side. That's where the voices I'd heard were coming from. They were even louder now. Half a dozen people in blue scrubs were scrambling around a figure lying in bed.

"Get the damn line back in!" someone shouted.

A woman crossed in front of the door, momentarily blocking my view. When she moved, I saw Toby—the man who'd passed us coming down the hall—standing over the figure on the bed, trying to hold him still.

The figure on the bed started writhing from side to side, screaming louder now, something wordless, inarticulate.

He was too far away for me to see his face, but the voice—harsh and guttural though it was—I recognized.

It belonged to Dominick Cazale.

Juarez appeared again, suddenly wearing a mask and latex gloves. He moved to the open door. A stocky Asian man in a blue shirt and khakis intercepted him.

"Doc," the man began, "do—"

"Not now, please," Juarez said curtly. He pushed past the man and into Cazale's room, sliding the door shut behind him.

It was suddenly quiet.

Movement in one of the rooms to my left caught my attention. I turned and through the panel saw a woman helping a young boy walk from his bed to a huge steel bathtub that took up almost half of the room. The boy was wearing a see-through black T-shirt and matching pants.

His right arm below the elbow was gone. Above the elbow, his arm was a mass of reddish black swollen skin.

The woman turned then and smiled at me.

I smiled back.

She turned away and began peeling the T-shirt off the boy. His skin underneath looked pink, and new.

I walked forward till I was standing next to the man in khakis, who had taken up position just to the right of the door to Cazale's room. He was looking through the panel, into the room beyond.

I looked too.

Everyone was still clustered around Cazale's bed; from the set of their faces, it was plain they still didn't have the situation under control. Juarez stepped forward, gesturing to Toby, who hadn't moved from the position I'd seen him in earlier, behind Cazale at the head of the bed, holding his shoulders down.

Toby moved now, stepping back from the bed. Juarez took his place. I saw his mouth moving, his hands making calming gestures as he leaned over Cazale.

Juarez held out his hand to a nurse who had appeared at his side. She put a needle in it.

All hell broke loose.

Actually, it was Cazale who broke loose. Somehow—I found out later—he found the strength to tear off the restraining strap holding his left arm to the bed. It had prevented him from moving while he was in a coma, to let the skin the doctors had so painstakingly sewed on have a chance to bind to his body.

In a few scant seconds, he undid the work of weeks.

The strap ripped away, his left arm was suddenly free. He struck out at the nurse next to Juarez. She fell back. Cazale pushed himself up on the bed with his free arm, trying to get to his feet.

For the first time, I got a good look at what the fire had done to his face.

It was bad, Juarez had said.

No. It was worse.

The entire right side of his head was swollen; the skin was red and raw-looking. So was his scalp: the fire had burnt away all his hair, save for a small patch on the left side of his head that stuck up now like an unmown patch of lawn.

His right ear was gone without a trace.

So was the right side of his nose, replaced by a clot of scar tissue, maroon against the pinkish magenta skin of his face. Blood oozed from a crack in the scar tissue now, dripping down in a straight line, like an arrow pointing toward the corner of his mouth, which was frozen into an unnatural grimace.

I took all this in in the span of a heartbeat. And just as that heartbeat ended, Cazale looked toward the door and met my gaze.

The look in his eyes was one of almost unimaginable agony. I doubt that he recognized me, much less any of his surroundings.

The figures in blue closed in front of him again, and he disappeared.

Toby stood at the head of the bed again, holding Cazale's shoulders down. Juarez approached, still holding the needle, his expression grim. This time, he wasn't making any attempt to calm Dominick down.

He plunged the needle into his arm.

A nurse pushed an IV cart over to the bed. A plastic hose dangled from the cart. Juarez picked it up and attached the end to the needle he'd stuck in Cazale's arm.

A minute passed.

The nurse at the cart stepped back from the bed, her face twisted in distaste. She crossed to a sink at the far side of the room and peeled off her gloves. They were wet and shiny.

Not with water, I realized suddenly.

With blood.

"Jesus, what a freaking mess," the man next to me said.

He was seeing the same thing I was: now that Cazale had stopped struggling, my eyes wandered over the rest of the room.

There was blood splattered on the floor.

Blood on the bedclothes.

Blood all over the gloves, gowns—and in some cases, even the masks of the medical personnel in the room.

Later, I would discover why.

When Cazale had been admitted to the hospital, his burns were so severe that the first thing they'd done was to perform a procedure called debridement.

Put in layman's terms, what they do is cut away the dead skin, layer by layer, going down, down, down, until the patient starts to bleed. Then the doctors know they've reached living tissue.

Then they could take the skin from undamaged areas of the patient's body to replace what had been lost. They'd started it already, Juarez had told me. But the skin hadn't been attached long enough to bond.

And Cazale's struggles had twisted it all off.

They would have to start all over again.

Cazale's struggling had stopped now.

Juarez stepped back from the bed and wiped his brow with the back of his elbow.

Blood smeared across his forehead.

A nurse came and wiped it away; then she laid a hand on his elbow and whispered something into his ear. He turned and looked first at me, then the man standing next to me at the door. His face hardened. He said something to the nurse; she turned and said something to Toby.

He came to the door and opened it.

"Doc says you two got to wait out there," Toby said, pointing around the corner toward the reception area.

"Ask him when we can talk," the man next to me said.

"He's busy," Toby said. "He'll come out and talk to you later."

"Ask him—"

"He'll talk to you later," Toby repeated. "Now you got to go."

He slid the door shut behind him.

"That is what they used to call the bum's rush." The man next to me smiled and stuck out his hand. "Nicholas Yamana."

I shook it.

"You a friend of Cazale's?" He didn't even wait for me to answer, just kept talking. "Poor old guy. You think he just lost it?"

"Sorry?"

"The fire, I mean. You heard that he started it, right?"

"Yeah," I said. "I guess I heard that."

"So what's your theory? Why'd he do it?"

I shook my head. "I haven't got a clue."

"Come on. Everybody's got a theory, right?"

I looked at the man again. "You're the policeman."

He held up his hands. "Guilty as charged." He offered up a half smile. "Sorry. Should have told you right up front, I guess, but people have a habit of clamming up once they realize they're talking to a cop. So—what do you think? What made him set the fire?"

"I'll tell you, Officer, I—"

"Detective."

"All right . . . Detective Yamana, I don't think he did do it. Dominick Cazale was not the kind of man who—"

"You're wrong." Yamana smiled up at me in a way I found instantly infuriating. I could see why Juarez wouldn't want to have anything to do with this guy. "We've got all the evidence we need to convict him. The gas can with a partial fingerprint, the place he stood, the matches he used. The only thing we don't know is why."

I shook my head. "I can't help you there. You could show me all the evidence in the world, and it still wouldn't make sense to me."

Yamana shrugged. "Maybe you know something that would help me understand the circumstances a little better. When was the last time you talked to him?"

"A couple months back."

Someone tapped me on the shoulder.

I turned and saw one of the nurses glaring at me.

"You two are really going to have to leave. Now."

"Hey, no big deal," Yamana told the nurse. "Walk with me awhile, will ya?"

Suddenly I was tired: I wanted nothing more than to be out of the hospital and relaxing out in the sun. But I was a long way from being able to do that: I had to find a room for tonight, and that was not going to be easy this close to Miami, I'd been told. I planned on picking my car out of the hospital parking lot and driving north along the ocean. Hopefully I could find a motel with a vacancy, cable TV, and a short stretch of beach.

Everything else would have to wait a little bit.

"Detective, maybe we can talk later. I've been up since—"

"Hey, I just need a few minutes of your time. The sooner the better for your friend, okay? Come on, I'll buy you a cup of coffee."

I shook my head. "Coffee is the last thing I need right now."

"How about a beer, then, huh? Come on, what do you say?"

"Detective." I stopped walking and turned to face him. "I have no idea what could have made Dominick Cazale set that fire, all right? Now if you'll excuse me—"

"Maybe a better question is why he wanted to kill his wife."

I shook my head. "He didn't want to kill his wife, Detective. He loved—"

"He tied her to a chair, splashed gasoline all around her, and lit a match. Does that sound like love to you?"

For a moment I couldn't speak.

"That's ridiculous."

"It's the truth."

"No. No, I don't believe it."

Yamana shrugged. "It doesn't matter what you believe: it's what can stand up in court. And we have evidence that can stand up in court."

I looked in his eyes and knew he was telling the truth.

Somebody tapped me on the shoulder again.

I turned and found myself staring into the angry eyes of the same nurse who'd told us to leave earlier.

"You have to—"

"All right," Yamana said. "We're going."

He grabbed me by the arm. I followed, too tired to put up any resistance.

chapter four

Yamana led me to a Days Inn not far from the hospital. No beach, but cable TV and a pool. I checked in and met Yamana at the bar.

The man was relentless: the second I sat down, he started back in, picking up right where he'd left off.

"So how well did you know the wife?"

I rubbed my eyes, wishing for a second I'd stayed in my room. "I never met her."

"When Cazale talked about her, what did he say?"

"We didn't really talk about her, that's what I'm trying to tell you."

"He never mentioned her at all?"

"He did, but—"

"Just tell me what he said. It'll help me get a picture in my head of the two of them together. How they related to each other. Right now, I got nothing."

So I told him what I had learned about Mary Cazale: how she and her husband had met, where they'd lived and traveled, how they'd both been in public education all their lives.

"Christ, they worked together *and* they were married?" Yamana shook his head in disbelief. "That would do it for me, I'll tell ya. Right around the bend." He shook his head again. "Can you imagine, my wife on the job with me? Holy Christ."

I didn't know what to say to that. I didn't know his wife at all. I was already developing a great deal of sympathy for her, however.

"Still . . . that's not a good reason to kill somebody, is it?"

I glared at him. "That's not funny."

"Sorry." He shook his head. "I'm always saying stupid stuff like that. Ignore me. It's just when you see this kind of thing a lot, you develop a thick skin about it."

"All right."

We were both quiet for a moment: not exactly a companionable silence—I would rather have been a million other places—but it felt good to be sitting in a comfortable chair underneath something other than fluorescent lighting.

"Detective, how sure are you about this—that Cazale did what you said?"

"One hundred percent, I'm sorry to say. Listen, I wish it was otherwise. My first thought was that it was an insurance thing—you know, an old couple, running short on cash, they decide to burn down their house for the insurance money. It made sense, given the circumstances. They bought the house—really, it's a bunga- low—back in the seventies for about seven grand. Now it's worth six figures."

"But it doesn't look that way now?"

"No. We got a look at Cazale's bank accounts, and they're doing all right. And then, we put together the crime scene and . . . well, you don't want the gory details, take my word. And you definitely don't want to see the pictures."

I nodded. I'd seen enough of what fire could do to a human being earlier today.

"Anyway . . . ," Yamana said. "Tell me about the last time you talked to Cazale. How long ago was it?"

I took a deep breath. I was thirsty and hungry: I suddenly realized I hadn't eaten since the plane flight this morning.

I wanted a beer.

I raised my hand to get the bartender's attention.

"What, you need something? Hey, buddy!" Yamana shouted.

The bartender, who was at the opposite end of the bar drying glasses and putting them into a wooden rack above his head, looked up. "I'll be with you in a minute."

"I'll take a Coke," Yamana shouted, ignoring him. "And my friend here will have a . . ." Yamana turned to me expectantly.

I studied the row of bottled beers on the top shelf behind the bar. "I'll have a Beck's," I said.

"Beck's!" Yamana relayed.

The bartender glared at us.

Yamana turned back to me. "So . . . that last time you talked to Cazale . . . tell me about it. How did he sound? Different? Like he might be under a lot of stress for some reason?"

Reflexively, I started to say no, that the Dominick Cazale I had met last Thanksgiving was a calm, dignified man, happy and content with his life. I pictured the two of us in the little booth at the front of the Corner Bistro, exchanging histories.

And then I remembered that the two of us had talked once since then.

And Cazale hadn't been quite as content.

It was June 22: I remember the exact date because I was walking out the door to a friend's surprise party when the phone rang.

"Hello?"

"Hey, it's Dominick. Hope this isn't a bad time."

"No, no," I said, glancing at my watch. I had a few minutes. "What's new? How've you been?"

"All right, I guess. Still kicking."

"That's good. Better that than the alternative."

"Right." He let out a short laugh. It sounded forced, unnatural.

In New York, he'd had the energy of a man twenty years younger. Now . . . I could hear every one of his eighty-five years in his voice.

"So, Dominick . . . what can I do for you?"

"Well, I was reading your book," Cazale said. I assumed he was talking about *The Blair Witch Project Dossier*, which he had cooperated with me on for publication. "And I had something I wanted to ask you about. You got a few minutes?"

"Well." I glanced at my watch. I didn't. "Actually, I'm running late for something. Let me call you back, all right?"

"Sure."

"You going to be in tomorrow afternoon?"

"Got nowhere else to go."

He laughed again: the same forced sound he'd made before. "Dominick . . . is everything all right?"

"Sure," he said quickly. "Everything's great."

He was lying: but I didn't have time to pry the truth out of him. "All right then. I'll call you tomorrow," I said.

But I didn't: I forgot to call him until a week or so later. I got his voice mail. I left a message. A week later, when he still hadn't returned the call, I phoned again.

This time there was no voice mail . . . which is when I decided to phone the police.

"So he sounded tired to you?" Yamana asked. Our drinks had finally arrived; Yamana picked his up from the bar and took a sip.

"And just not himself. Every other time I talked to him—"

" 'Every other time.' How many times did you guys talk in total?"

"Half a dozen, I'd say. But that time we met in the city, that was really the only time we talked about personal stuff."

"So you got no clue what might have been bothering him?"

"None." I picked up my beer and drained half of it in one gulp. "Can I ask you a question now?"

"Sure. Shoot."

"Anybody else you've talked to give you a reason why Cazale might do this?"

"No. In fact, you want to know something interesting?" Yamana turned on his stool to face me directly now. "You're only the second guy I've met who's spoken with him in the last two months. What do you think about that?"

Yamana's gaze bore into me now, and I suddenly got the feeling that maybe the detective was a little sharper than he seemed, that the constant chatter and obnoxious behavior was something he could turn on and off like a switch.

"I don't know what to think about that," I told him.

"Yeah. I don't either." Yamana's gaze drifted. "Cazale and his wife are the king and queen of Hallandale Beach up until two months ago, then they fall off the map. Stop seeing their friends, stop going to movies, stop showing up at the Lychee Garden for the early-bird on Sunday. They pretty much stop leaving the house, from what the neighbors say. Only time they seem to get out is to buy groceries, and go to church on Sunday."

"So the priest," I said. "Maybe he knows something."

"He's the other guy who spoke with Cazale—and he won't tell me a thing."

A sudden thought occurred to me. "Maybe it was a suicide pact. Cazale was supposed to die too in the fire."

"So that's why he tied her up? That doesn't sound like any kind of pact to me. Besides, if you're gonna kill yourself, there are a lot less painful ways to do it."

I couldn't argue with that.

"We thought of the medical angle too," Yamana went on. "She has some kind of terrible disease, he wants to end it for both of them. But her medical records say she's fit as a fiddle—for an eighty-eight-year-old, anyway. And again, the whole fire thing . . . it just doesn't make sense. If you want to put someone out of their misery, why put them through that much pain?"

I couldn't understand it either. "So maybe there's something wrong with the picture of the crime scene you've got. Maybe—"

Yamana shook his head firmly. "No. No, no, and no. I'll go get the pictures, if you want."

"You don't have to. It's just that I can't believe—"

"No. Don't go there. You sound like Dr. Juan."

"Dr. Juarez."

"Juarez. You talk to him, the guy was a saint. Never did a thing wrong in his life."

"Well, maybe it's true."

"Uh-uh." Yamana drained his Coke with a loud slurping noise, then held up the glass. "Yo! Bartender. Refill down here." He turned to me. "You want another?"

"Sure."

"And a Beck's!" he yelled, grabbing my glass and holding it high. "Thanks."

The bartender brought the drinks. Yamana drank from his, rolling an ice cube around in his mouth. "Look, if there's one thing I learned doing this job, it's that everybody's got a skeleton in their closet. Somewhere, sometime in their life, everybody did something they'd rather nobody in the world knew about. This guy Cazale, I'm sure he's got a skeleton all his own rattling around somewhere. When I find out what it is"—Yamana picked up his glass and drained it—"I got the feeling I'm going to find out why he killed his wife."

He stood. "I gotta get back to headquarters. Everybody's gonna wonder where I've been." He took a big wad of bills out of his pocket and peeled off a twenty.

"Hey, buddy!" he yelled. The bartender visibly grimaced.

Yamana waved the bill in the air, then set it down on the bar. "This is for you, all right? Thanks!"

"And here . . ." He held out a card. "If you think of anything else that might help, call me."

"I will." I took out my wallet and put the card in it. "Thanks for the beers."

"You're welcome," he said. "I'll see you."

He left. I sat alone at the bar for a few minutes, nursing my beer and wondering what in the world would drive a man to do what Cazale had.

Skeletons in the closet, Yamana had said. I thought, Burkittsville, Rustin Parr. Those might be a good place to start.

I suddenly felt like Sherlock Holmes, hard at work on a case. The only difference was, my powers of detection were usually only good in a library.

"You want another?" The bartender was standing over me.

I looked and saw I'd drained my glass again without realizing. "No. I'm all right, thanks."

The bar around me was starting to fill up; so was the restaurant. It was getting on five-thirty.

I went upstairs to my room, intending to order room service.

First, though, I called the hospital. Juarez had left for the day, so

I had the operator put me through to his voice mail. I left him my number at the motel and asked him to call me with news of Cazale's condition. Then I checked my own voice mail and found a few West Coast calls I had to return.

By the time I finished doing that, the bed looked more inviting than the room service menu.

I was asleep before the sun went down.

chapter five

I woke up the next morning with an empty stomach and a head full of questions. A Waffle House down the road solved the first problem. I took A1A south into Hallandale Beach, hoping to take care of the second.

I'd gotten Cazale's address from the white pages in my hotel room. Yellow crime-scene tape marked the lot where his house had stood. White sawhorses—PROPERTY OF HALLANDALE BEACH POLICE—blocked access to the lot from the sidewalk.

All that remained of the house was a pile of debris and blackened timber. You could tell what it had looked like, though, by the houses on either side of it: Yamana had been right to call them bungalows. Square, flat-topped one-story buildings, with virtually no front yards, and a narrow strip of concrete running between each that doubled as a driveway.

The house to the right of Cazale's had also been damaged by the fire: black soot ran down the exterior wall next to that driveway. Some of the shingles on that side of the house had recently been replaced.

Something else about that house caught my eye: a small statue of the Virgin Mary in the front yard. I got out of my car and knocked at the front door.

I heard someone approaching the door, the sound of a peephole being uncovered.

"Yes?"

"Hi. I'm a friend of the people from next door, and—"

The door opened, revealing a little, blue-haired old lady in an orange and white housedress.

"Oh my goodness, Dominick and Mary, it's horrible. What happened to those two . . . it's the worst thing. The worst."

Her name was Shirley Ward; she and her husband had lived next door to the Cazales for fifteen years.

She invited me in to talk. We sat in her living room, around a coffee table cluttered with pictures of what I assumed were Shirley's children and grandchildren. The room was cluttered too: more pictures, and dozens of little porcelain statues. There were blue and white angels, Mary and child, the three wise men, Jesus on the cross, Jesus with his hands clasped together praying.

Mrs. Ward offered me red-and-white-striped peppermints from a candy dish. I declined and turned the conversation back to the Cazales.

"How well did you know them?" I asked.

"Oh, we were great friends." She crossed the room to a shelf full of pictures, and pulled one down. "Here. This is from a fishing trip we took a few years back."

The four of them were posed side by side in the stern of the boat, leaning on a guardrail. Shirley stood between Dominick and another man, whom I recognized from pictures on the coffee table: her husband. On Dominick's left was another woman: Mary Cazale. This was the first time I'd seen her.

She was a striking-looking woman: slim, sharp-featured, with fashionably cropped silver hair.

Fifty years ago, she must have been quite a beauty.

As if she'd been reading my thoughts, Shirley spoke. "She was such a beautiful person—outside and in. I don't like to think about what happened to her too much. It gives me nightmares."

"I can imagine."

"Tell me—how is Dominick?"

"Well . . . he's doing much better than they expected. And the prognosis for his recovery is very good." Not the complete truth, but not a total lie, either. Juarez had stressed to me how much of a miracle it was that Cazale was still alive. And I didn't think it would do much good for Shirley Ward to hear a recap of what had happened in the hospital yesterday.

"Oh, that's wonderful news!" She clapped her hands together. "A lot of people around here will be so glad to hear it. Now . . . how can I help you?"

"A simple question, really." And I asked it.

As I suspected, she not only knew the answer, but gave it to me without a second's hesitation.

I got halfway out of my seat, intending to go. Then I thought of another question: "Did you notice anything different about the Cazales these last few months?"

"I should say so. They never left their house."

"Any idea why?"

"No. I remember when it started, though. They'd gone away for a few days, over the weekend, and when they came back . . . well, everything was different. We were supposed to play bridge—we had a regular bridge date, every Tuesday night—and Dominick called to cancel. He said Mary wasn't feeling well. I went over a few days later to see how she was, and they wouldn't even come to the door." Shirley shook her head. "It was just so strange. The two of them used to have people over all the time. They were so involved in the community, then, all of a sudden, they were living like shut-ins."

I remembered Yamana's words: the king and queen of Hallandale Beach.

"Did you ever ask them what was the matter?"

"Oh, I tried, believe me. I called on the phone, they never answered, I went to their house more than once, and . . . oh, I just didn't understand it. Fifteen years we were friends, and she wouldn't say a word to me. I felt so bad."

"And no idea why?"

"No, but whatever it was, I think it had something to do with Mary. Dominick was the only one that I ever saw leave the house after that weekend: he did the shopping, he came out to get the mail every afternoon, and he went to church on Sunday. He always went to church." She looked up at me. "But we've talked about that already, haven't we?"

I nodded. "That we have."

I thanked her for her time and left.

Back in the car, I wondered if I was going about this the right way.

I could have asked Yamana straight out for the information I wanted, rather than snoop around Cazale's old neighborhood looking for it. But then the detective would want to know what I wanted the information for—and I wasn't sure I had an answer for him.

So for now, my course of action was set.

Shirley Ward had told me the Cazales attended church at St. Luke's, two blocks inland, off Hallandale Beach Boulevard.

That's where I was headed next.

The church was five minutes away, a stone building set well back from the road behind an immaculately maintained lawn. I parked on the street and followed a flagstone path up to and past a sign exactly like the one I'd seen in front of every other church I'd been to in my life. Black sign, white letters, behind a piece of glass. Today the sign read:

ST. LUKE'S CHURCH

Mass Saturday 6:30

Sunday 9, 11, 1

Psalms 1: 2

But his delight is in the law of the LORD

And in his law doth he meditate day and night.

Father Terry J. Callahan, Pastor

A red pickup truck was in the driveway next to the church; the path led me past it and up to a separate building: the rectory. I went inside.

To my left was a paneled room with a long wooden table. Four elderly women sat at it, folding stacks of pink paper into flyers and stapling them.

One looked up as I entered. "Can I help you?"

"I hope so. I'm looking for Father Callahan."

"He's upstairs with the contractor." She pointed to a stairwell down the hall. "Just follow that to the second floor and turn to your left. You'll find them soon enough."

I did: as I reached the top of the stairs, I heard voices off to my right. They got clearer as I got closer.

"We'll want to wire all the rooms that way—is that possible?"

"Well . . . what I would do is give you a big enough box so you had room to add whatever you needed later. I'll run conduit so that's easy to do."

The entire upstairs, I saw, was being renovated. Drywall was up but unpainted, electrical outlets were wired but uncovered, and the ceiling was a mess of open ducts and dangling wires.

The voices I heard were coming toward me. A second later, two men—one short, heavily muscled, with a red bandana tied around his head, the other, taller, thin, in a priest's collar—walked past an open doorway in front of me.

I cleared my throat. "Excuse me?"

Both men turned. The priest said, "Can I help you?"

"Are you Father Callahan?"

"That's me."

"Sorry to interrupt. The woman downstairs said you were up here. I wonder if I could have a few minutes of your time. I'm a friend of Dominick Cazale's."

"Of course." The priest turned to the other man. "Richard— would you mind?"

"Not at all." The other man pulled out a tape measure. "I've got to finish measuring for the fixtures anyway."

"Thanks," said the priest. "I'll be right back."

He led me downstairs and around the back of the church to a fountain, with stone benches set in gravel all around it. We sat.

"What a beautiful day," he said. "It seems a shame to be cooped up inside."

"It looks like a big project you're working on."

"It is. We've been talking about redoing that top floor for years, so we can get the Sunday-school children a classroom with windows. Now we're finally doing it."

"Congratulations."

"Well, I lose out in the deal—my office gets smaller," Callahan didn't look—or sound—too upset. "Not that I really mind—I do some of my best work right here, anyway."

Callahan looked to be about my age—early forties—with thin, reddish brown hair that was receding from his forehead, and wire-rim glasses that kept slipping down his nose. He had a kind face, and a kinder voice. The kind of voice you'd want to confess things to.

"So you're a friend of Dominick's?"

"I am."

"You must be a fairly good friend, to have come all this way to see him."

"I suppose so," I said, suddenly realizing that Callahan was right. It was a hell of a flight to make for somebody that I had only met once and talked to half a dozen times.

This was the first chance I'd had to really think about why I'd done it.

"He's a good man," I said. "And from what the doctor was saying, it sounded like he needed help."

Callahan nodded. "Have you been to see him?"

"I was at the hospital yesterday. He's out of the coma, you know."

"Yes. Doctor Juarez called a few days ago and told me. They think he's going to be all right." Callahan looked at me a moment. "How did he seem to you?"

I met Callahan's gaze. I hadn't intended on telling him what had happened yesterday at the hospital. I saw no point in upsetting him, just as I had seen no point earlier in upsetting Shirley Ward.

But like I said, he had the kind of voice you wanted to confess things to.

"The poor man," he said when I'd finished. "He's been so troubled these last few weeks."

"That's why I wanted to talk to you, to find out why."

And then I realized there was something else I had to tell Father Callahan: the truth about the fire.

Even before I finished that story, he was shaking his head.

"No. I simply don't believe it."

"That was my first reaction too."

Callahan got up and started pacing. "Let me tell you something. We feed the homeless breakfast here every morning. A few years back, the neighborhood got up in arms about it. Thought we were introducing an undesirable element to the area. You know who saved the program? Dominick. He went door-to-door for us for a solid week, up and down these streets. That's the kind of man he was."

"I know that."

"Not the kind of man who would set his own house on fire," Callahan said emphatically. "Or kill his wife." He studied me for a moment. "But you think he did it now, don't you?"

I nodded.

"What changed your mind?"

I told him what Yamana had told me, what he'd offered to show me from the crime scene.

Father Callahan pursed his lips. "But why? What could possibly have been in Dominick's mind to make him do such a thing?"

"That's what I wanted to ask you. According to the police, you and I are the only two people who talked to him recently."

"Ah." Callahan sat down again. "I begin to see. You want to know what we talked about."

"I do."

"Angels, believe it or not. Angels and devils."

"I'm sorry?"

"Nothing. It doesn't matter." Callahan shook his head. "I couldn't help that detective, and I can't help you. When Dominick and I talked . . . we talked under the seal of the confessional. Do you understand?"

I did: conversations that took place under the seal of the Catholic Church were not only private, but legally privileged. Whatever information had passed from Dominick Cazale to Father Callahan was going to remain between them.

No wonder Yamana had sounded frustrated.

"I'm sorry. I wish I could help you, I really do." Callahan stood again. "I have to get back upstairs. You say Dominick is conscious: get him to tell you what we talked about. Or get him to agree that I can tell you: that's the best I can do. "

He held out his hand; I stood and shook it.

Then I watched him go.

Talk to Dominick: that sounded eminently reasonable.

But it wasn't going to work. I'd seen Cazale yesterday, Father Callahan hadn't. Lengthy conversations with Dominick were not going to be possible anytime soon.

"Father Callahan!" I called after him. "Just tell me this much: Did Dominick ever mention the name Rustin Parr?"

The priest stopped in his tracks. "Well," he said, keeping his back to me, "that's a name I wouldn't have expected anyone around here to know."

"I'm not from around here."

"Yes." He turned to face me.

We stood there for a moment, looking at each other.

"Please," I said.

He sighed. "Dominick did an interview about that person— Parr—for a news program. That was when he came to me for confession."

Callahan turned and without another word walked back into the church.

It didn't matter: he'd confirmed the ugly suspicion that had been lurking in my head since yesterday afternoon.

Whatever drove Dominick Cazale to set the fire that killed his wife, Rustin Parr was at the heart of it.

chapter six

Back at the Days Inn, I picked up messages.
One on the hotel's voice mail was from Juarez, apologizing for abandoning me yesterday, suggesting that I come back to the hospital during visiting hours that afternoon. Cazale was sedated, but awake and aware of his surroundings. "It might be good for him to see some familiar faces," the doctor said.

Several messages were on my home voice mail. The only one I had to return was from Federal Express, who had a package they were trying to deliver to me. I called them back and told them I was in Florida for a few days, then left the address of the Days Inn. I made a few other calls: to the hospital, telling Juarez I'd be there in a few hours, to a friend back home canceling a dinner date for the weekend, and finally to room service for some lunch.

Then I sat down to think about what Father Callahan had told me.

Cazale had given an interview on Rustin Parr for a news program: my first guess was that he'd done it for one of the local stations. I called the news division at one of them and spent half an hour trying to track down somebody who might be able to help me.

And then I realized that I was wasting my time.

If the program had something to do with the Blair Witch, I already had a source who might know about it.

＊　　＊　　＊

Bill Barnes was a retired librarian who lived in Burkittsville. By unofficial consensus, if not actual appointment, he was the town historian, and spent his days organizing (and often reorganizing) the vast collection of artifacts belonging to the Burkittsville Historical Society. Most of those artifacts were Civil War mementos: remnants of the supplies, ordnance, and everyday gear carried by the soldiers—both blue and gray—who'd passed through Burkittsville during the war. Lincoln himself had visited Burkittsville to visit the wounded. The society's most valued possession was a brief note the president had written to Colonel Winfield S. Hancock, urging him to keep his spirits up.

Barnes had happily shown me the note when I visited the town a few years back; it occupied the center position in the room's only display case.

But the material relating to the Blair Witch was his pride and joy. The society had a newspaper article from 1825 relating the drowning of Eileen Treacle. It had a *McCrory's Illustrated* from 1886, with an article and accompanying sketches and photos discussing the ill-fated search party sent out to rescue Robin Weaver. And it had a little rag doll that had once belonged to Emily Hollands, before it turned up in the basement of Rustin Parr's house.

No one on earth knew more about the legend of the Blair Witch than Bill Barnes. Which was why I suspected he might know about the program Cazale had been interviewed for.

He did; in fact, he'd been interviewed for it as well.

"It was called *The Burkittsville 7*," he said. "Only it wasn't a news special, it was a documentary about Rustin Parr, made by a public TV station out of—let me think a minute, here—ah, Dayton, Ohio, I believe. This fella who did it, though—he had some kind of ax to grind. When I saw it, I was sorry I'd let them put me on. I didn't agree with what that program was trying to say, not one little bit. This man, his theory was that Parr didn't kill those little children."

Which was the rough equivalent of saying that Charles Manson had been falsely accused.

"You're kidding," was all I could think to say.

"Wish I was," Barnes said. "And are you ready for this?" I could almost see him shaking his head. "You know who he says did the killings, this filmmaker? Kyle Brody."

"A twelve-year-old kid killed seven other children?"

"That's what he says."

Now it was my turn to shake my head. "He's got evidence of this?"

"Evidence?" Barnes snorted. "Who needs evidence? What he's got is a bunch of hooey about exactly what Parr said to the police, and some close-ups of that writing on Parr's house. Bunch of nonsense." Barnes was silent a moment. "Tell you the truth, the only part of the whole program that I bought into were the interview pieces with the priest—the ex-priest, sorry. The man comes right out and says Rustin didn't do it."

Now that was strange. Over all the years, Dominick had steadfastly refused to breathe a hint of what Parr had told him during his confession.

"I'd like to see this tape," I said.

"Well, it was a public TV station out of Dayton, Ohio, did it, like I said. You might give them a call."

After I hung up with Barnes, I did just that. I was in luck: the woman I spoke to at the PBS station in Ohio tracked down a copy for me at the Fort Lauderdale PBS affiliate. I made another call and, after much pleading (and a promised exchange of money), arranged to see it later that day at their offices.

Then I headed back to the hospital.

I went directly to the waiting room in the burn center; Juarez came out to meet me. He looked as if he'd had a rough night: dark circles under his eyes, another day's worth of stubble on his beard.

"Hey." Even his voice sounded tired. We shook hands. "How are you?"

"I'm good. How's Dominick?"

"Calmer than the last time you saw him. Which isn't surprising, considering the amount of morphine being pumped into his system right now." Juarez sighed and ran a hand through his hair. "All that thrashing around yesterday pretty much undid the work we'd done over the last two weeks. We had a long night fixing him back up."

"You didn't sleep at all, did you?"

"I grabbed a couple hours." Juarez smiled. "Come on back, you can see him."

We started down the hallway.

"Sorry to have to get you out so quickly yesterday," he said over his shoulder, "but—"

"Hey, no need for apologies. I saw what was going on."

"You talked to that cop."

"Yeah."

"Did he tell you his theory about the fire—how they think Dominick started it?"

"He said it wasn't a theory. He said the evidence at the crime scene was pretty undeniable."

We turned the corner and entered the burn unit proper.

It was as quiet today as it had been chaotic yesterday: the only sounds were the buzz of the fluorescent lights overhead, the soft murmur of nurses and doctors consulting with each other, the distant thrumming of machinery.

"I'm no expert," Juarez said, "but I have a hard time believing you can reconstruct a crime scene when a place gets burned to the ground."

What he said made sense. But then, I wasn't an expert either.

We stopped at the door to Cazale's room.

"Remember what I told you yesterday?" Juarez asked.

"Don't stare. Don't look away either."

He took two surgeon's masks from a tray and handed one to me. We both put them on.

"That's right," Juarez said, his voice muffled by the mask. "And don't forget he's drugged: if he tries to talk, it probably won't make much sense. And we don't want to get him excited again, which means don't talk about the fire, all right?"

I nodded.

Juarez clapped me on the shoulder. "Good. Then let's go."

He slid the door to Cazale's room open, I stepped inside.

Dominick lay motionless on his bed, encircled by machines. Some displayed blinking green numbers, others carried fluids to and from his body through clear plastic hoses of differing sizes.

A white sheet covered his body; only his arms and head were visible. A black band of cloth restrained his left arm at the wrist. I had no doubt that the rest of his body was somehow immobilized as well. Juarez slid the door shut behind us with a soft click. I approached the bed.

This time I was prepared for what I saw: the disfiguration, the scarring, the red, raw look of the skin. The eyes were different, though: the caged, hunted look I remembered from yesterday was gone, replaced by a dreamy, drug-induced tranquillity.

"Does he even know where he is?"

"He's responsive." Juarez stepped in front of me and up to the bed, on Dominick's left side. "Hello, Dominick."

One corner of Cazale's mouth curled slightly.

Juarez motioned me forward with his hand. "Let him see you."

I moved closer: Cazale's gaze shifted and came to rest on me.

"Look, he knows you're here." Juarez took my hand and guided it on top of Cazale's. "Say something to him."

I smiled down at Cazale.

His head shifted. I couldn't be sure if he had done it consciously or not. His gaze continued to track me.

"Dominick." I smiled as best I could under the circumstances. "It's good to see you."

This time he definitely reacted: the corner of his mouth curled again.

Scar tissue cracked underneath his nose; little drops of blood appeared.

"Easy," Juarez said, blotting the blood with a gauze pad. "Easy."

I tried to think of something besides banalities to say to Cazale, but drew a blank. What I really wanted to talk about was Rustin Parr. "The doctor says you're doing good, you're going to pull through. We're all glad, Dominick." I smiled again.

His left hand shot out and clamped on my wrist.

"Mary," he whispered. "Mary."

"It's okay," I said. "Everything's okay."

His head moved, ever so slightly, from side to side. "No. Iss not okay." His voice sounded guttural, harsh—unused.

"Easy, Dominick," Juarez said. "You're in the hospital. Everything's going to be fine. But you need to stay calm, give your body a chance to heal."

"Mary?" he said again, and this time I understood the word as a question.

He was asking about his wife.

I looked up at Juarez, who had moved to the other side of Dominick's bed. He shook his head, meaning, don't tell him. Don't tell him anything.

"Easy, Dominick," the doctor said. "Save your strength."

Cazale's grip on my wrist tightened, the tendons on his neck bulged.

"Mary?" he repeated, his voice growing louder.

"I don't know where he's getting the strength to do this," Juarez said, almost to himself. He turned and adjusted a knob on one of the machines. "I'm upping the morphine."

Cazale's left arm strained against the bonds; the loose gown he wore slid down, exposing his forearm.

Something was burned into the skin there. Scar tissue, but formed into a pattern of some kind: I caught just a glimpse of it before Cazale slumped back in his bed.

The pattern looked vaguely familiar.

"That's enough of this." Juarez glared at me as if I were somehow at fault. "You'd better go."

I reached down and pried my hand free from Dominick's, one finger at a time.

"I have to leave, Dominick," I said. "I'll be back."

His head lolled to the side again: the morphine was doing its job.

But Cazale wasn't going off to dreamland without a fight: his eyelids drooped, but his gaze remained fastened on mine as I left the room.

The tranquil expression he'd worn earlier was gone.

chapter seven

I had been in the waiting area for only a few minutes when Juarez came storming down the hall toward me.

"What were you doing in there? I thought I told you not to upset him."

"Me? I didn't do anything. He just—"

"What did you say to him?"

"You were right there—did you hear me say anything?"

"Christ." Juarez threw up his hands and began pacing back and forth. "One of the grafts ripped: we have to operate again."

"I'm sorry."

Juarez shook his head. "His system can't stand much more of this."

He needed a target for his frustration, and I was it. I understood, and tried to give him the benefit of the doubt: he was tired, he was concerned for his friend. So was I.

"Did you see those markings on his arm?" I asked.

My change of pace threw Juarez off. "What?"

"The markings—on Dominick's left arm? What are they?"

Juarez looked at me as if I'd grown another head. "What the hell do you think they are? They're burns."

He was still angry. And he wasn't the only one.

Coming through the double doors of the burn center reception area, with a full head of steam up, was Detective Yamana.

"There he is." Yamana put his hands on his hips and glared at me. "Dick freaking Tracy."

The detective started yelling: What did I think I was doing? Why was I going all over the city asking people questions? Who did I think I was? Was I trying to get a job with the Hallandale Beach Police? Maybe he should call Inspector Luger and offer to give me his job — and so forth. I couldn't get a word in edgewise.

Juarez let him rant for about thirty seconds, then broke it up. "I have to get back to my patient. And you two have to leave."

He chased both of us out of the burn center. From the look he gave me, I had a feeling it was the last I was going to be seeing of the doctor — and Cazale — for a while.

Yamana, on the other hand, wouldn't leave me alone. "So did you find out anything interesting? Anything that might be worth sharing with the detective in charge of the case?"

"Look, Detective, I'm just trying to understand what happened."

He'd followed me all the way into the hospital parking lot. We were standing in front of the white Dodge Neon I'd rented. I had the keys in the door lock; he had a hand on the driver's side door to prevent me from opening it.

"And do you now? 'Cause I sure as hell don't."

I shook my head. "I don't either, if it makes you feel any better."

"It doesn't. And you wanna know why?" He jabbed a finger at me: I thought he was going to poke me in the chest. "Because I have the feeling that you" — he jabbed the finger again — "know something you're not telling me."

I was tempted to reply I knew a lot of things I wasn't telling him.

"I'm not sure about anything," I said. "Plus . . . what I do know, I'm not sure you'll want to hear."

He considered that a moment. When he spoke again, I was dealing with the kinder, gentler Detective Yamana I'd glimpsed briefly the day before.

"There's nothing I don't want to hear about this case. About Cazale. Look, I want to understand what happened here as much as anybody."

Now it was my turn to consider.

"All right," I replied finally. "Remember that thing you said yesterday—about skeletons in the closet?"

"Sure."

"Well, Cazale's got one."

Yamana nodded. "Of course he does. And you know what it is."

"That's right."

He took his hand off the car door. "Speak."

I looked at my watch. It was one-thirty. I was supposed to be at WPFL—the Fort Lauderdale Public TV station—in half an hour.

"Take a ride with me," I said. "I'll do better than that."

Yamana and I ended up taking separate cars to WPFL's offices—a two-story, pink concrete structure on Hollywood Boulevard, about twenty minutes north of Hallandale Beach. We met in the building's lobby; a security guard called our names in to the woman I'd spoken with earlier. She came out to the lobby to meet us.

"I'm Meredith Blake, public relations." She shook our hands in turn.

Yamana held hers a moment longer than necessary. "Charmed."

She ignored him and held out a videocassette. "Here it is. Come on back: we'll set you up in a viewing room."

"We really appreciate your doing this," I said.

"Not a problem. You have good timing. We were going to archive this next week—in a big warehouse clear across town. We're a little tight for space here."

She wasn't kidding: we had to navigate around cardboard boxes piled two and three high as we made our way down the hallway.

"We were supposed to move two years ago," Meredith said. "And then—hey, Pete!"

In the hallway ahead of us, a man in blue coveralls was pulling a cart with a TV monitor and other equipment on it out into the hallway.

"Hold on a minute—where are you taking that stuff?"

"Sponsorship meeting upstairs," Pete said. "They want to see the new commercials."

"But I need it."

"Sorry." He finished pulling the cart out into the hall and began pushing it away.

"How about Edit Two?" Meredith asked. "Is that free?"

He shook his head. "Nope."

"Edit Three?"

"Nope. Nobody's in the screening room, though."

"Very funny." Meredith frowned and turned to me with an apologetic look on her face. "I'm sorry about this. Do you guys want to come back later?"

"Just give us the tape," Yamana said. "We'll find a place to watch this."

"I can't do that. It's our file copy."

"You can trust me," Yamana replied.

She shook her head.

"That guy said something about a screening room . . ." I began.

"It's a joke," Meredith said. "It's not really a screening room."

"Is it someplace we could watch the tape?"

"I suppose so . . . ," she said hesitantly. "But—"

"Well, then," Yamana said, "lead on."

The so-called screening room was the size of a small closet; in fact, I suspected it had been a closet not too long ago. Now a TV monitor and consumer VCR were built into the far wall. Meredith had to show it to us from the corridor: all three of us would never have fit in there at the same time.

"We usually just use this room to check copies," she said. "You sure you guys don't want to come back?"

I looked at Yamana. He shrugged and said, "We'll manage."

"Then here you go." She handed me the tape. "Leave it at the front desk when you're finished."

There was just enough room for the two of us to stand side by side in the closet. I inserted the tape into the VCR and pressed play.

"What is it exactly we're seeing here?" Yamana asked.

"A documentary Cazale did a couple months back. Something called *Burkittsville 7*."

"Burkittsville?" Yamana squeezed past me and hit the stop button on the VCR. "We're talking about Burkittsville, Maryland?"

"That's right."

"They went there a couple months back. Cazale and his wife. Flew up to D.C. on a Friday and rented a car. It seems to have been the last place they went before going into hibernation."

I remembered what Mrs. Ward had said: they'd gone away for a few days, over the weekend, and when they came back . . . well, everything was different.

Something had happened in Burkittsville.

"So what's so special about this place?" Yamana asked. "Why did they do a documentary on it?"

I hit the play button. "Watch."

Forewarned as I had been by my conversation with Bill Barnes earlier in the day, I was still surprised by the filmmaker's obvious bias. *The Burkittsville 7* was all about the 1941 killings—but the man's blatant disregard for the physical evidence against Rustin Parr, his obsession with poor Kyle Brody, and the way he skimmed over or ignored every piece of the puzzle that didn't fit into his point of view . . . well, it wasn't what I expected.

It definitely wasn't what Yamana had expected either.

Standing side by side in that small space, our shoulders touching, I couldn't help but be aware of his mutterings and sidewise glances, which increased in frequency when the documentary's producer—Chris Carrazco—came on the screen and began going over the legend of the Blair Witch in detail.

A few minutes into the tape, Yamana had had enough. "That's it. I got better things to do with my time than this."

The detective turned sideways in the small room, partially blocking the screen, where Bill Barnes was puttering around the Burkittsville Historical Society and talking about his childhood in Burkittsville—and growing up under the shadow of Rustin Parr.

"Do me a favor," Yamana said. "If there is ever another time when I invite you to share your thought processes with me—and I don't think there will be, but just in case there is—please disregard that invitation, all right?"

He squeezed past me and out into the hall.

Dominick Cazale came on the screen and started talking.

Yamana peeked his head back around the corner.

Dominick looked exactly as he had when we met in New York; he even, unless I missed my guess, was wearing the same suit and tie.

He could pass for a man in his sixties. Strong, solid-looking, in complete possession of his physical and mental faculties.

And yet . . .

He was nervous about something.

It showed in the way he answered Carrazco's questions: sometimes he was evasive, sometimes confrontational. Especially when it came to what Parr confessed to him that evening in November 1941. The thing that Dominick had kept private for so many years.

The screen filled with images now of a much younger Cazale, with Rustin Parr. A photo flashed: the crowd gathered to watch Parr swing from the gallows. The camera cut back to Cazale being interviewed, present day: he began ranting against the entire world for demonizing Rustin. The sense of unease I'd felt watching him before intensified.

I had told Yamana earlier that the Dominick Cazale I knew was simply not the kind of man who would deliberately burn down his house—much less cause the death of his wife.

I still believed that, and yet . . .

Cazale, as he spoke, was hiding something.

The film cut to an older woman: Janine Brody, Kyle's sister. She started talking about Rustin Parr's trial.

"Cazale was a priest?" Yamana shook his head. "Nobody I talked to knew that."

"I don't think he liked to broadcast the fact."

"Because of this Rustin Parr guy?"

"Detective, can we talk about this later?" Carrazco had pulled out a whole collection of Rustin Parr memorabilia now, most of which was from Carrazco's private collection: a picture of Parr with his twin brother, transcripts from the man's trial. Most of it, I had never seen before.

"You think he's going to be on again?"

I started to answer when the image on the screen caught my attention: Carrazco had pictures of the 1941 killings.

I'd seen them before: shots of the woods, the run-down house, the staked-out graves in the basement where the missing children's bodies had been found.

And of course, the writing that had been found on the walls of Rustin Parr's house, after the killings.

That writing filled the screen now. Runic inscriptions, Carrazco called them. From a language called Transitus Fluvii. More commonly known, he said, as the witch's cipher.

I recognized the runes as well.

I'd seen them burned into the flesh of Dominick Cazale's arm earlier that afternoon.

chapter eight

We have no way of knowing what the runes originally meant. The Inquisition saw to that: in murdering hundreds of thousands of those who practiced the religions that predated Christianity in Europe, the Church murdered those religions as well. Thousands of years of accumulated knowledge—folklore, history, spiritual wisdom—gone in a relative flash. Among the casualties: an understanding of the two-dozen-odd symbols that, taken together, are commonly known as the witch's cipher.

Scholars have managed to agree on a few salient points regarding this cipher.

Number one, it was written right to left, and backwards.

Number two, it was never an everyday language: its usage was ceremonial and associated with the more powerful magics of witchcraft—a rite of healing, a spell intended to insure good luck, a change in fortune . . .

A curse.

Number three, the act of writing the script in and of itself was said to put you in an altered state of consciousness, make you more receptive to signals from other dimensions.

The use of the script, in other words, was intended to open a door.

✳   ✳   ✳

The documentary continued to run. I had trouble giving it my full attention, however: the images on the screen kept morphing into the ones running through my head.

Symbols carved in stone: symbols burned in flesh. The runes at Rustin Parr's house: the scars on Dominick Cazale's arm. One and the same. Undecipherable.

On the monitor, twelve-year-old Kyle Brody had grown into a confused, shattered man. Black-and-white film of his years in the sanitarium flashed past: shots of him eating, raving, almost attacking the camera.

The idea of him as a killer grew more plausible.

The documentary had Yamana's full attention now; from occasional interjected comments, I could tell he was buying into the argument Carrazco was making.

Dominick did indeed appear again, at the end of the documentary, when he raised his eyes to the heavens and wondered how Parr—much less God—could ever forgive him for breaking the vows he had made.

And then he told Carrazco that Rustin Parr, who had gone to the gallows on November 22, 1941, as one of the most hated, reviled men of the twentieth century, was a gentle soul, incapable of violence. That Parr had told him in his final confession that he had killed no one.

The screen faded to black.

"So that's the skeleton in Cazale's closet, huh?" Yamana asked.

I nodded.

"Helluva skeleton," Yamana said. "More like a whole freaking graveyard. But I don't see what it's got to do with the fire."

"Cazale feels guilty about Rustin Parr. About keeping silent all these years."

"So that makes him suicidal. That far, I can get. But—" Yamana looked me in the eye. "What does all this have to do with his wife?"

"I don't know." Which was true, but the pieces of the puzzle were beginning to come together in my head, at least a little bit. "Can I ask you a question?"

"Sure."

"How did you know Cazale and his wife went to Burkittsville?"

"Credit card bills: some stuff we salvaged from the fire. Why?"

I smiled. "I thought you didn't want the benefit of my thought processes anymore."

"Leave out the process. Just give me the end product."

"Fair enough. Then show me what you found in their house."

He considered. "Why?"

"I'm trying to put myself in Dominick's head. To figure out what he was thinking when he set that fire. I think Burkittsville's got something to do with that."

Yamana nodded. "Can't do any harm, I suppose. You'll tell me if anything rings a bell with you?"

"I will."

"All right," he said, squeezing past me. "Then let's get out of this closet and head downtown."

I took the tape out of the machine and followed.

"Like I told you, we weren't able to salvage much," Yamana said. "Just a couple boxes of stuff: the place was pretty well trashed."

The evidence room, in the basement of the Hallandale Beach Police Station, was cavernous, with aisle after aisle of metal shelving stacked high with white corrugated boxes and sealed plastic bags. Thick masking tape labeled with big block letters identified the contents of each shelf. Fluorescent lights crackled and dimmed overhead; every sound we made echoed on the bare cement floor.

Yamana marched me over to a plain wooden table.

"Sit," he commanded, pulling over a chair. "I'll be right back."

I did as I was told.

Yamana returned a moment later with two cardboard boxes. He set one on the floor, and the other in the center of the table. "I'll spread everything out," he said. "Don't touch a thing. Let me know if there's anything you want a closer look at, and I'll handle it. Understood?"

"Understood."

"And let me know your thought processes."

"Is that a joke, Detective?"

He smiled. "Wiseass."

Yamana began pulling things out of the box. Some pictures: a younger Dominick and Mary, posing in front of what looked like a

South American village. A head-and-shoulders portrait of Mary, alone. A similar shot of Dominick. There was a wooden music box, and a snow globe that said SAN DIEGO on the inside. A framed letter from the archbishop to Cazale, expressing regret at his decision to leave the priesthood.

A stack of mail: different catalogs, some brochures, and, of course, bills.

"Here's their last Visa statement. Look." Yamana opened the envelope and unfolded the paper inside. "You can see when they were in Burkittsville," he said, running his finger down the page.

Yamana was right: it was easy to follow the course of their trip from the itemized list of charges: the Avis Rent A Car at Dulles, the Colonial Diner in Hyattstown, a Holiday Inn at Frederick. The next day, two charges in Burkittsville proper: W. W. Smith's General Store and . . .

"'The Blair Witch Walk?' I asked. "What's that?"

"A tour group. Apparently this Blair Witch is a big tourist attraction."

"I can believe that. What else?"

"Hold on a minute." Yamana placed everything carefully back into the first box and brought out the contents of the second. This one seemed to be full of things from the Cazales' bedroom: some sweaters, a pair of shoes, a dress, and a pile of books, pages singed on the outside. Most were paperbacks: mysteries, women's fiction. Two, slightly larger than the rest, caught my eye.

"Can I see those?"

Yamana handed them over without looking at them.

They were library books, I saw at a glance, with Dewey decimal numbers written on white labels taped to the spine.

One—a yellowing softcover volume of no more than a hundred pages—was called *Maryland Folk Legends and Folk Songs*, by George G. Carey. I leafed through it, impressed: it was oral tradition, set down on paper, recollections and reminiscences of stories and songs generations old. I made a mental note of the author and title, then turned to the other volume.

It was a thick hardcover, called *Witchcraft: Primal Persecution*.

I didn't need to leaf through it to see what was inside: I knew every one of its five-hundred-odd pages intimately.

I'd written it.

"He was reading my book."

"What?"

"This is my book." I held it up so Yamana could see my name on the spine.

"Let me see that." He reached across the table and snatched it out of my hand. He began flipping through it. "The last time I talked to him, Cazale said he was reading my book. I thought he meant a different one." My mind was racing now. The book Yamana was holding was the first thing I'd written, my senior thesis expanded over four years into a full-length study of witchcraft through the ages: its historical evolution, its most famous strongholds, its spells, its languages, its most famous practitioners, its most notorious enemies.

Yamana was still flipping pages. "Jesus Christ," he said, shaking his head, "you don't really believe all this crap, do you?"

"It's not a question of what I believe. It's what Cazale was thinking about while he looked at this."

"The Bible."

"What?" I looked up and noticed Yamana had stopped flipping pages, and was instead studying one rather intensely.

"What he was thinking about." Yamana held the book open and laid it down faceup on the table. Then he slid it across to me. "See for yourself."

I looked at the page Yamana had opened to. It was a dictionary of the known runes associated with Transitus Fluvii—the witch's cipher. Drawings of the runes, and my best guess at their associated meanings. The entire right side of one page was filled with pencil scrawling.

I Samuel 28:15
Isaiah 6: 6-7
I Corinthians 3:15
Mark 8:36, 37
II Thessalonians 1:8

And so on. An entire page full of biblical citations.

"How do we know Cazale wrote these?" I asked.

Yamana took the book from me and flipped to the inside back cover. "Well, the last time somebody checked out this book was 1981." He flipped back to the page of runes and pointed again to the pencil scrawls. "Pencil would have faded a lot more than this in twenty years."

He was right.

"So what are these references?" Yamana asked.

"Biblical scholarship is not my forte, but one of those looks awfully familiar."

I took the book back from him and flipped through until I found what I was searching for. "Here. Look."

The page I'd turned to reproduced a woodcut from sixteenth-century Germany, depicting a woman being burned at the stake.

I read the caption underneath it out loud: "Second Thessalonians one:eight. 'In flaming fire take vengeance on them that know not God, and that obey not the gospel of our Lord Jesus Christ.' This biblical passage was justification for the death of thousands of innocents during the Inquisition."

Yamana was silent a moment. I could see the wheels in his head turning.

"So these other citations here—"

"I'd have to look them up."

"Sure. But they're related, they have to be."

"I agree."

"So what?" He shook his head. "This guy burns up his wife because the Bible tells him to? No, that's a rhetorical question, don't answer it."

I didn't, because I was too busy working through the solution to a different one in my mind.

Out of the five-hundred-odd pages in my book, why had Cazale chosen the one about the witch's cipher to write those biblical references on?

I thought of what I'd seen at the hospital.

Symbols carved in stone: symbols burned in flesh.

The answers were beginning to come together.

Yamana gave me a photocopy of the page with the biblical references. I told him I'd look them up and call him back.

I did indeed drive directly back to the Days Inn and go to my room, where I pulled out the copy of the Bible the Gideons had so thoughtfully placed in the drawer of the night table next to my bed. Then I set it aside, picked up the phone, and dialed Maryland information.

"Burkittsville, please," I told the operator. "Something called the Blair Witch Walk."

I didn't like going behind Yamana's back like this. At the same time . . . I had the feeling I was going places he would never visit in a million years.

"Hi. This is Rick, and you've reached the offices of the Blair Witch Walk. If you're interested in one of our tours of historic Burkittsville and the Black Hills, please leave your name and number at the tone and we'll call you back. We regret that our overnight trips are sold out through the summer. Please book your reservations now so we can assure you a space in the fall. Thank you for calling, and—"

Someone picked up the phone.

"Hello?" It was a man. He sounded out of breath. "Hold on a minute."

While he wheezed, I explained who I was, and why I was calling.

"Oh, yeah." He sounded younger than I'd first thought, a college kid probably, working a summer job. Not the voice on the recording. "I remember those two. Took them around town myself. Weird couple."

"How so?"

"Well, to start off with, it was like eighty degrees out, and the guy was wearing this long coat and a hat. Like he was in disguise, or something."

Or, I thought, as if he didn't want anyone to recognize him. Which only made sense: even today, there were probably people in Burkittsville who would run Dominick Cazale out of town on a rail if they knew he was there.

"Where did you take them?"

"Wow. Let me see now. Hmmm. I think we went to the cemetery first, right off Main Street. Then down First, then to Town Hall, then—"

"Whoa. Slow down a minute. What did they look at?"

"Where?"

"At the cemetery."

"I don't know. I wasn't paying that close attention."

"All right. Then you took them to First Street, you said?"

"That's right."

"And there . . ."

"Sorry, man. That's not even a usual stop on the tour. It's just a bunch of people's houses, pretty much."

I sighed and made a mental note to myself.

If I ever wanted a tour of Burkittsville, I was not going to give my business to the Blair Witch Walk.

"To be honest with you, I don't know why they needed a guide: the guy seemed to know his way around pretty well. Even when we went out in the woods, to the old Rustin Parr house."

A chill went down my back.

"Guy musta stood there for a solid ten minutes, just staring at the place. And when his wife started walking around inside the foundation walls—wow, man. He just freaked out."

"Anyplace else you took them?"

The man thought a moment. "Not after that. He just wanted to get back into town. Say, why do you want to know all this stuff?"

"Just trying to get a couple things straight in my head. You've been a big help."

"Well, all right. Glad to be of service."

I hung up and called the hospital.

I wanted to see Cazale's arm again.

Juarez wasn't there. As I was leaving a message on his voice mail, someone knocked on the door.

I covered the mouthpiece. "Just a minute!" I yelled.

I asked Juarez to call me when he had a moment, then I went to answer the knock.

A young woman in a red and blue Federal Express uniform wanted to know if I was D. A. Stern.

"That's me."

"Then I've got a package for you. Sign here, please."

I did, and she produced a large manila envelope that someone had tried to feed to a paper shredder.

"We're refunding the shipper's money on this one," she said. "And I have to apologize: this kind of thing almost never happens with our packages. It went to the Memphis hub by mistake and, for some reason, sat there for two weeks." She handed me the package. "It's kind of funny the way it turned out: this goes clear across the country and ends up right back where it started from."

She pointed to the label.

The package had been mailed from Hallandale Beach.

It had been sent by Dominick Cazale.

I don't remember thanking her.

All I know for sure is that I had the envelope open before the door was closed.

Inside was a leather-bound journal.

When I opened it, a batch of photographs fell out. They were crinkled and yellowing around the edges. Mixed in with them was a piece of paper.

It was a copy of an old newspaper: page 10 of the May 4, 1941, edition of *The Washington Post*. I skimmed it quickly.

An article in the lower right-hand corner caught my eye: something about a suspicious fire in the woods near Hagerstown, Maryland.

I picked up the journal and began reading.

The
Journal
of
Dominick Cazale

Burkittsville c. 1939

chapter nine

> The Lord is my shepherd: I shall not want.
> He maketh me to lie down in green pastures: he leadeth
>   me beside the still waters.
> He restoreth my soul: he leadeth me in the paths of
>   righteousness for his name's sake.
> Yea, though I walk through the valley of the shadow of
>   death I will fear no evil: for thou art with me; thy rod and
>   thy staff they comfort me.

The Psalm of David: it's a beautiful passage. My favorite in the
Bible. Through all the days of my life, I have sought—and
found—comfort in its recitation.

   Tonight, though . . .

   My wife is in the next room, too frightened to sleep.

   And try hard as I might, I don't see anyone here but me.

2:30 A.M.

Midnight used to be the witching hour.

   It was an ungodly time of night to be awake, back before

electricity. People needed to be up with the sun in those days, to get all their work done. That's the way it was in Burkittsville.

Anyone out past sundown was shiftless, no-account—up to the devil's work.

Mary finally fell asleep, so I snuck out to the grocery down the street for a sandwich. There, I saw a woman out with her little girl, who couldn't have been older than six. Two-thirty in the morning, and the child was still awake. No good can come of that.

June 3
Noon

Mary is calmer this morning. She wants to watch television, to see what's happening in the world outside.

Which I suppose is a good thing, because it gives me time to write all these things down that I'm thinking about.

Although, looking back over the first few pages here, I realize that late at night is not the time to start a journal.

So let me begin again.

My name is Dominick Cazale.

In my life, I've been a priest, a teacher, a civil rights activist, and a social worker. I've tried to help people, you could say. What else are we put on this earth for, after all, but to love and comfort one another?

End of sermon.

What I suppose I am now is a guardian.

Which is how Rustin Parr described himself to me, once upon a time, in a town called Burkittsville, Maryland.

That's where Mary thinks all the trouble started.

In a way, she's right.

Though from where I sit, it really began back in Baltimore.

Which is where this journal should really start.

In 1961, after Mary and I were married and had settled down in Mexico for what we thought was the long haul, after Joe left the force for good, after Vince Jr. and Donna had made their move to

New York City, we all flew back to Baltimore Mother's Day
weekend to surprise Mom.

She'd long since sold the old house and moved into a two-
bedroom apartment in what we would've once called the fancy
part of town, but which we now saw as no more than her due.
The doorman wanted to call up and announce us; Joe insisted,
somewhat forcefully, that he do no such thing.

The look on Ma's face when she answered the door and saw
her three sons standing there dressed to the nines . . . I will never
forget it if I live to be a hundred.

We took her out for dinner at a nice Italian restaurant right
across the street and then drove all the way to Rondelli's, in the
old neighborhood, for cappuccino and cannoli.

The whole night, she just kept eating and smiling, eating and
smiling, while me and Vince and Joe kept arguing about the Yankees.
I was outnumbered as usual: the turncoat New York acolyte squeezed
in between two Senator fans. The girls—Joe was with someone that
year whose name, God forgive, escapes me at the moment—were
talking amongst themselves as well, Donna and Mary probably
passing along stories about Vince and myself that we thought were
intimate secrets. I have to admit we all did a pretty good job of
ignoring my mother, who we were supposedly there to fete.

We ignored her for a good long time too, until the girl who'd
been serving us came over and asked if we wouldn't mind paying
our check because she was cashing out. Which was when we
looked around and realized that no one was left in the café but us.

We settled the bill jointly, the girls excused themselves to the
ladies' room, Vince and Joe went to redeem our cars from valet
parking . . .

And that left me and my mother sitting alone at the table.

"I hope you had a good time tonight, Ma."

She nodded, then reached across the table and patted my
hand. "It's all like a dream, Dominick."

I put my hand on top of hers. "No, Ma, it's no dream. We're
really here."

She shook her head. "I don't mean tonight. I mean—my
whole life. It's all been a dream."

Home . . .

"I don't understand."

"Well, it all runs together in my head now. I look at the three of you, and you're grown men, but I can see you like you were as little children, back in the house in Woodbury. You remember that house?"

"Ma, how could I forget the house? I spent ten years of my life there."

She smiled and sighed. "Oh, we had such good times there. I see you and your brothers playing cowboys and Indians in the backyard, and your father coming up the sidewalk from work, and the four of you running around the living room—"

"With you yelling at us to stay off the furniture, don't forget."

My mother, who usually thought I was God's gift to comedy, ignored me completely.

"I see you coming back from mass with your cassock all folded neatly over your arm. I see Joseph sneaking up to his bedroom after breaking curfew. I see Vincent and that singing teacher of his . . ."

"Mr. Layden."

"Mr. Layden, yes, I see the two of them at the party we had the night of Vincent's senior glee club performance. Do you remember that?"

I did remember that. I remembered sitting in the audience and being absolutely amazed that my big brother could sing so well, while they made me stand in the back of the church chorus and only move my lips.

"I remember" was all I said.

"And I see myself too, as I am now, as an old woman—"

"You're not old, Ma."

"As an old woman," she repeated. "And as a bride, as a little girl, and they don't seem any different to me, those places." She leaned closer. "Fifty years ago, twenty years ago, yesterday, tonight . . . they all run together in my mind, just like in a dream, where you can move around from one place to another, from one moment in your life to another, without it taking any time at all. Do you understand?"

A horn honked outside: it was probably Joe, who had all the

patience of a child suddenly plopped down in front of a Christmas tree full of presents . . . which is to say, none.

"Life is just a dream, Dominick." She struggled to her feet.

"It passes, and then we wake up."

I helped her on with her coat. "And then what?"

She smiled at me over her shoulder. "You were the priest. You should have the answer to that one."

All the way back to her apartment, I thought about what my mother had said, and about the things that had happened in my own life, all the good, and the bad. Sometimes it did seem they all ran together; being back in Baltimore after so many years away only intensified that feeling.

That night, after Mary fell asleep, I took one of the cars we'd rented and drove downtown, to the corner of Park and Eager, to the site of the old Park Bank building. Where on November 10, 1932, my father had gone to work, closed the door to his office, put a gun to his head, and shot himself.

A few nights before that, at dinner, Mom had been yelling at Joe for some transgression or other. He had, as usual, been yelling back, when to everyone's surprise, my dad, who usually let his wife have the first, last, and all intervening words when it came to disciplining us boys, interrupted her.

"Connie," he said, putting his hand on her arm, "let me say something here."

She was too stunned, I think, to offer a word of resistance.

"Joe," he said then, with a gravity to his voice that he never had around the house, "did you do it?"

I can't even remember what "it" was now, to be honest.

"Dad, first of all—"

"No excuses, Joe. Did you do it?"

He nodded. "Well, sure, but—"

"All right, then." My dad picked up his fork and started eating again. "The wheel will turn."

We all looked at each other: no one had any clue what he was talking about.

He pointed his fork at me, then. "Dominick, here, will back me up on that. Am I right, Dom?"

"Sure, Dad," I said immediately, still wondering what he meant.

"The wheel will turn. It does a man no good to walk away from the wrong he's done. Own up to it, Son. Own up to it." Dad put down his fork then and stared down at his plate. "Because life has a way of paying you back for your sins."

And then my dad started to cry.

He was really talking about his own troubles, of course, which in that fall of 1932 were the whole country's: banks closing, businesses failing, whole families living out on the streets, going from town to town looking for work, looking for food. We all knew about them to some extent, my mom more than the rest of us, I'm sure. It was in the papers: the Park Bank's officers were the subject of a criminal investigation. People had lost their life savings; someone had to pay.

That someone was going to be my dad.

Life paying you back for your sins, he said.

As I am being paid back now.

Sometimes the details are hazy to me; sometimes they're so real, so immediate, it all seems like it happened yesterday. The things I did and didn't do, the things I wish I had done. I see the continuum of my own years, my growth from boy to man, the path that took me from priest to teacher to husband, from Baltimore to New York to Hallandale, and so many places in between. At last I understand what my mother was saying that night so long ago: life is just a dream.

No part of it more so than those three years I was assistant pastor to Monsignor Joseph Fannon at the parish of St. Joseph's, the years that I have kept locked up in the attic of my mind for so long . . . the years of Burt Atkins, and Albert Collins, and Damon Bowers. Of Horace Gersten, and Peter Durant, and the Brody family: Michael and Carol, Janine, and her poor brother, Kyle.

And of course . . . Rustin Parr.

Those years, so wonderful and terrible when I lived them, now seem to me like a story I was read as a child, or a fairy tale spun whole from the stuff of imagination.

A haze hovers over my memory, rendering entire portions of

those times—faces, places, names, and dates—formless and indistinct.

Still, there is one thing I do recall with unfailing clarity: the sweet smell of lilacs, wafting through the warm spring air.

Bushes of them lined the road as I drove into Burkittsville for the first time on May 6, 1939. Father Fannon had grudgingly lent me the use of his brand-new black Ford—"It had better come back without a scratch on it or you'll be riding a horse next time," were his exact words—which was a pleasure to have running full throttle on the new macadam of U.S. 340, as all the driving I'd done previously had been on the crowded streets of Baltimore, in cars that wheezed and clunked every inch of the way.

It was a beautiful Saturday afternoon, perfect for a drive through the rolling hills of Frederick County. I passed fields of wheat and corn, fenced-in pastures where I caught glimpses of cattle and sheep, all the while skirting the edges of the forest that grew thick along the gentle slope of South Mountain.

And then, just as the sun was going down, the macadam vanished, the road became gravel, I rounded a corner, and there before me was a sign.

WELCOME TO THE HISTORIC VILLAGE OF
BURKITTSVILLE, 1824

The date, I assumed, marked the village's founding—though looking at the town laid out before me, all wood and stone, its only concession to the industrial revolution a filling station and a big red sign that said MOTEL—it could just as easily have stood for the current calendar year.

That motel sign was my destination: the Burkittsville Motor Lodge. Easy to spot, as the man I'd talked to on the phone promised.

I parked the car and walked in.

Two men were behind the front desk, their backs to me, hunched over a big piece of furniture that I realized, as I drew closer, was a big Philco radio.

"Come on, Burt, let's just go listen at Charlie's," one said.
"We'll miss it."

"You, Albert, are a nervous Nellie." They had the radio pulled
away from the wall, I saw, and the back panel off. Burt knelt down
and reached a hand into the chassis. "Ah. There's your problem,
see. One of these tubes here is loose."

"I sure hope you know what you're doing."

"I always know what I'm doing. Here. This ought to—"
With a little click the radio suddenly jumped to life.
Senators-Tigers, top of the eighth inning.

"What'd I tell you?" Burt slapped the back of the radio back
on, put his hands on his knees, and stood. "Now run over to the
store and get us a couple beers to enjoy this with."

I cleared my throat. "Excuse me."

Both men turned.

"You must be Father Cazale," Burt said.

"Now what gave me away, I wonder." I fingered the collar
around my neck.

"A priest with a sense of humor. I like you already, Father. I'm
Burt Atkins. Welcome to Burkittsville." He clapped the other man
on the shoulder. "This here's Albert Collins. He runs this place
for me. Say hello to Father Cazale, Albert."

Collins smiled—I got the feeling that if Atkins had told him to
carry me up the stairs, he would have done that as well—and
stuck out his hand.

"Pleased to meet you, Father. Your room's right upstairs. I'll
show it to you."

"No rush." I nodded toward the radio. "What's the score?"

"No score yet," Atkins said. "You like baseball, Father?"

I smiled. "Went to seminary right around the corner from Babe
Ruth's old stomping grounds."

"Ah. Your team of choice would be the Senators as well,
then—am I right?"

"No, actually. Yankees, if you can believe it."

"Yankees? How in the world did that happen?"

"Sheer spite," I answered. "My older brother liked the
Senators."

Michael Guidry

"So what do you think about Gehrig then, Father?" Collins chimed in. "Is he through?"

"About Gehrig?" I shook my head. "What about Gehrig?"

"You didn't hear?"

"Look at his face, Albert, of course he didn't hear." Atkins frowned. "Gehrig sat down last weekend. He didn't play."

"You're kidding."

"Took himself out of the lineup," Collins said.

"I don't believe it."

I couldn't believe it. All right, so Gehrig had had a subpar season the year before, and he wasn't getting any younger, but still . . .

The Iron Man had played in over two thousand consecutive games. Since Calvin Coolidge was president. Pretty much since the day I'd become a Yankee fan.

Lou Gehrig, sitting on the bench?

In retrospect, I should have taken it as an omen.

chapter ten

Not that it would have made any difference in the way my life turned out, but I would have liked the chance to say mass in English once. To be able to look into the eyes of the parishioners I was bringing God's grace to and know that they heard and understood what I was saying.

Those of you born in the Catholic faith the last quarter of this century will have no idea what I'm talking about. But the others among you, who can remember when your prayer books were in Latin and great portions of your Sunday mornings were spent staring at the back of a priest's head, will take my meaning.

What brought all this on? you ask.

Well . . . today I went to church.

Mary had slept through the night without incident, the first time in two weeks that had happened. When I finally decided to wake her, at a little before ten, she opened her eyes, smiled up at me, and asked if I wouldn't mind going out and getting the paper for her to look at.

For a moment, it was as if none of this were happening.

We had a Sunday morning like the Sunday mornings we used

to have. We read the paper, and watched *Meet the Press*, and bemoaned that the most intelligent people in the country never, ever ran for elective office. I made pancakes.

"Dom," Mary said to me, "why don't you go to the one-o'clock mass?"

So I did.

And when mass was done, maybe a dozen of us remained standing on the steps outside the church, including Father Callahan, and a handful of my peers and friends. All of them were peppering me with questions about Mary's health, when the best time would be for them to drop by and see her. At the cost of a few bruised feelings, I managed to deflect each would-be visitor and avoid giving any definitive answers. And when, for a moment, the questions stopped, I pulled Father Callahan aside and asked him if we could talk in private.

"Of course, Dominick." We excused ourselves and went next door into the rectory.

"Sorry about the mess," Callahan said, leading me upstairs to his office. On the left side of the staircase the steps were lined with boxes; the second-floor hallway was filled with them too. "We're moving everything off the floor starting tomorrow, so . . ."

The rectory was being renovated, starting with Father Callahan's office, which was now practically bare: his books, photos, diplomas, et cetera, were all packed away. What remained in the room was a desk and two maroon leather chairs.

I sat at one, he sat at the other, and for a few minutes, we made small talk.

He asked if I was going to be working for the Future Foundation again that summer: I said I hadn't decided yet. I asked about the vacation to Greece he was taking to coincide with the renovation; he allowed that he was as excited as possible under the circumstances, "which are that I'm living my life out of boxes."

And then he asked what was on my mind.

"It's Mary, Father."

"Ah." He nodded. "I was afraid it might be that. A lot of people around the parish have been asking after her. Wondering what was the matter." He paused a moment, then looked me in the eye. "Missing her. I miss her too."

"I—we—understand that."

The question was in his eyes, and aching to escape from his mouth: What's the matter with her, Dominick? What's the matter with Mary?

"She's going to be fine," I lied. "It's only that we both would rather be by ourselves for the time being."

"Of course, and I've told people to respect your wishes, and leave you alone." Father Callahan smiled. "I don't suppose I've been entirely successful at doing that."

"Not entirely," I agreed, thinking mainly of our neighbor, Shirley Ward, who in the past few weeks had dropped off enough food on our doorstep to feed an army. "But I appreciate the thought."

"So what can I do to help?"

"Well . . . we've been doing a little reading together, in the Bible. Trying to come to terms with her illness."

He nodded.

"My biblical scholarship is not what it once was," I said, smiling. Father Callahan was one of the few people in my life who knew that I had once been a priest. "I was hoping you could point me towards some additional passages on the subject—some additional sources as well, perhaps."

"And what's the subject?"

I cleared my throat and told him.

His eyes widened with concern. "Dominick—are you sure you don't want to talk about this?"

"Really, Father—we're fine. It's nothing to burden yourself with."

"Now, Dominick, how long have we three known each other? Fifteen years?" He shook his head. "It's hardly a burden. Let me come to your house later this afternoon, talk to the both of you. We can—"

"No, Father, it's not like that. She's—I mean, to be candid, a lot of Mary's problem is in her head. That's why I thought talking things out with her a little more might help."

Father Callahan looked me straight in the eye for what seemed like an eternity.

I tried as hard as I could not to let the guilt I felt for lying to him show.

"I'll do what I can to help, of course," he said finally. He turned to the bookcase behind him and pulled down the one volume that remained on the shelves. "Just promise me one thing, Dominick. When you decide you do want to talk — anytime, day or night — you call me, all right?"

I nodded, and I promised.

1:30 A.M.

After a good day . . . a bad night.

Mary dreamt again of our daughter.

Her name was to have been Concetta Rosa Cazale, after my mother and Mary's grandmother. It was 1953, we were living in Morningside Heights, and something went wrong with the delivery. The doctor at St. Luke's wasn't able to save the child. He was barely able to save Mary.

But now — at least in the dreams my wife has been having these last two weeks — our daughter lives.

It was shortly after midnight that Mary cried out in her sleep, waking me up.

"It was the same dream, Dom," she said. I put my arm around her. "Connie is eight years old. She looks like my sister." I formed a picture in my own mind: a red-haired, gap-toothed, smiling child.

"We're at a lake somewhere, on vacation. You and I are lying on a blanket and Connie is swimming."

"If it's the same dream," I reminded her gently, stroking her hair, "you don't have to tell me the details."

But she did anyway. "She starts screaming. Because something is pulling her under the water."

"Easy now."

"We both run to save her. But when we get there — she's gone. Without a trace." Mary's voice cracked. "The water isn't even up to my knees, so where did she go? Where did she go?"

Tears ran down the side of her face and onto my hand.

"Shhh," I said, "it's all right."

"No! It is not all right! It is not all right at all!" Mary screamed, loud enough to wake the Wards next door.

I continued stroking her hair. Eventually her crying subsided and she fell back to sleep, snuggled up against me.

I wiped the tears away from her cheeks and touched the markings on her arm.

"It's some kind of fungus," Dr. Weitzmann had said when we went to see him. "I'm going to prescribe something for you that should clear it up in a few days."

June 5

1:00 P.M.

Witches, the Bible tells us, are about the devil's business.

They are the servants of Satan, his willing initiates, whose sworn duty here on Earth is to tempt man into acts of sin and wickedness.

Witchcraft itself is an "abomination" (Deuteronomy 18:10–12); "They who do such things shall not inherit the kingdom of God" (Galatians 5: 20–22); "Thou shalt not suffer a witch to live" (Exodus 22:18).

In the Middle Ages, these words were taken very seriously.

The Inquisition resorted to torture—the sawing off of limbs and/or breasts, the usage of stocks with iron spikes, the burning of various parts of the body—to elicit confessions from those it believed to be witches.

Most of whom were entirely innocent.

In 1628, one such man—Junius Johannes of Bamberg, Germany—managed to smuggle a letter to his daughter from his prison cell, shortly before he was executed.

"Now dear child," Johannes wrote, "here you have all my confession, for which I must die. And they are sheer lies and made-up things, so help me God . . . For they never leave off with the torture till one confesses something . . ."

He wrote this letter with hands that had been crushed by vises.

The point being that by the time the Inquisition finally drew to a close, those few true practioners of witchcraft left had developed a deep burning hatred for the Catholic Church and all who represented it.

The day after my arrival, I woke early and decided to say my prayers in a field at the edge of town. Before mass, I was supposed to meet the families of the parish at the motel, so I returned there to wait.

There was a little boy standing by my car, peering inside.

"Hello," I said.

The youngster turned to me and smiled. "Is that one of the push-button gearshifts?"

"It sure is."

"Yeah, I thought so. I've seen pictures of them in the magazines."

The boy managed to seem both intensely curious and completely bored at the same time. He looked to be nine or ten and had on a pair of dark trousers and a white T-shirt.

"What's your name, son?"

"Kyle. Kyle Brody."

"Ah." I nodded: the Brody family, I had been told by Monsignor Fannon, usually hosted the town mass at their house.

"Well, Kyle, I'm Father Cazale." I held out my hand, and we shook. "I'm going to be visiting with you this morning."

He was about to speak again, when a shadow passed across the two of us.

I turned around, and one of the biggest men I'd ever seen in my life was standing there. He must have been six and a half feet tall, and every inch looked to be carved out of solid muscle.

His size wasn't even the most fearsome aspect of his person though: that honor belonged to his face.

The entire left side of it was disfigured—the skin blotchy and purple, the features with a faint sag to them where they crossed that color line.

"I'm Michael Brody. That's my son." He looked at the boy with a faint expression of distaste, as if he couldn't quite believe the lad's patrimony himself. "He's not bothering you, is he, Father?"

"No, sir, he's not. He's just curious about the car." I smiled at Michael Brody and realized that at one time he must have been handsome.

The man scowled back. "I see you staring, Father, so I'll spare you the trouble of asking around. I got this"—he touched the side of his face—"working in the mines on the other side of South Mountain. One of the strikers hit a match at the wrong time, in the wrong place: fourteen men died, including both of my brothers. I guess you could say I was lucky."

I couldn't think of anything to say to that.

"Kyle!" the man yelled. "Keep off that car, y'hear!"

I turned and saw the boy, who had been leaning through the driver's side window trying to get at the gearshift, jump off and scurry away down the street.

Brody stared after his son and scowled. "Damn his ears, he never listens." He shook his head. "Excuse my language, Father."

"It's all right, Mr. Brody. And forgive Kyle. Boys will be boys."

"Aye, I suppose you're right."

"So I understand your wife has volunteered to have mass at your home this morning?"

Brody shook his head. "We had planned on it, yes, sir, but she's not feeling well." For the first time, an expression other than a scowl crossed his face. "We had a baby last week, a little girl."

"Well, congratulations, Mr. Brody."

"Thank you, sir. But Carol's feeling a bit under the weather today, I'm afraid."

"I understand. I'm sure we'll find another place to hold the mass."

He nodded.

"Will you be coming to mass today, Mr. Brody?"

"No, sir. I believe the sweat of a man's brow is what puts food on the table. But you'll see the boy—and my wife of course." He nodded curtly. "Good day to you."

And with that, he turned and walked away.

So the Brodys weren't at that first mass, but the Sullivans, the

Woodrings, and the Flynns were. We held it at the Flynns' farmhouse, and it went as smoothly as if we'd planned it that way all along. I gave a brief sermon on the importance of community, spent some time talking with the parishioners about their lives, and then drove back to Frederick, where Monsignor Fannon was so happy to see his car back in one piece that he gave me the next two days off, and I visited Ma in Baltimore.

The rest of those first few months in Burkittsville tends to blur together for me. I do remember spending a great deal of time with the Flynn family—John, Katie, and their twin daughters, Rebecca and Beth. I became friendly with Burt Atkins as well and found there was a little more to Albert Collins than I'd thought on first impression.

Mostly, during that time I got used to the rhythms of small-town living, the up-at-dawn, to-bed-at-dusk way that predominated among the people of Burkittsville, and the other Frederick County towns I served, a way of life geared to the family farms that most everyone in those towns lived and worked on.

Also, during this time I first discovered that sense of God that one finds only by walking the wide-open spaces of the natural world. The biggest patch of green I'd encountered growing up in Woodbury was the grass on a baseball field, so the idea that you could go out into the forest and see nothing but trees for miles and miles, that you could just keep walking and walking without seeing a railroad track or a paved road or even another person—it was almost inconceivable to me. So I began taking short hikes out into the woods, at first with John Flynn and later by myself. One of my great pleasures in those years was to drive out from the center of Burkittsville with a picnic lunch, park along Black Rock Road, and head off into the forest to commune with nature.

City boy that I was, I was just begging to get lost.

And one afternoon, that's exactly what happened.

Terra shelly

chapter eleven

It didn't take me more than ten minutes to know I was in trouble.

As I said before, I'm a city boy. Set me down at nine in the morning in Miami or Baltimore—or any big metropolis, for that matter—and by lunchtime I'll not only have found the best lasagna in a twenty-mile radius, I'll be on my second helping.

I can speak the language, is what I'm saying. But in the great wide open . . .

Well, maybe Davy Crockett could navigate without a compass or find an old Indian path by looking at the way the grass bent in the wind, but the only way I could get around was by paying close attention to the big blue splotches of paint splattered on the trees along the trail.

My usual routine was, pick up the trail at Black Rock Road and follow it into the forest for maybe fifteen minutes. That's how long it took to come to my little hideaway—a patch of grass on a gentle rise, with a nice view of the town below. I'd sit, unpack my lunch, and eat, hoping for a little wildlife to come along: a deer, a rabbit, even a squirrel would do. I'd share a little of my meal, then pack up and head back to my car.

Only this afternoon, as I walked down the rise, it didn't level off. It just kept going down. The trees got a little taller, the undergrowth a little thicker, and at some point, the blue splotches of paint vanished.

And then I came to a stream. In the half dozen times I'd been out in these woods, I had never seen a stream before.

"This is not good," I recall telling myself.

I hiked back up the hill, following the exact route I'd taken down, looking for those blue splotches of paint. Only when I got to the top, nothing was even remotely familiar about the terrain.

I took a deep breath.

Panic, I knew, was not an appropriate response. It wasn't that big a forest: I'd seen maps. All I had to do was get my bearings, and I'd be fine.

My biggest problem was that I was equipped for a picnic, not a hike.

I had no water in my knapsack. The first time I had told him I was going out in the forest, Burt Atkins had marched me into the general store (which, it turned out, he owned as well), and pulled a canteen down from the shelf.

"Buy it," he said.

I checked the price and told him that on a cleric's wages, a canteen was not an option at this time.

"I'll buy it for you, then," he said, and pulled out a wad of bills from his pocket.

I refused: the sin of false pride, in retrospect.

But now that I thought of that canteen, and the water that I didn't have, I remembered something else about water that John Flynn had told me once while we were hiking: "If you get lost, find running water and follow it. The towns in these hills grew up around the streams and rivers: they'll lead you back to people."

So I hiked back down the hill and started following the stream.

Going back to the stream also had one immediate plus: it gave me a ready source of drinking water. Which I took advantage of more than once as the hours passed and the shadows lengthened and the forest around me showed no signs of petering out.

Flynn had shown me a map of the Black Hills, and I wouldn't have thought I could've hiked for so long and not come to the edge of them. Still, not the end of the world. It was summer, warm enough even at night that, even if worse came to worst and I had to sleep out in the woods, I would be nothing more than a little sore when I made my way back to civilization, as I surely would the next day.

I undid my Roman collar, unbuttoned my shirt, and set off again.

My stomach was the part of me most upset at the thought of not returning home: it had been hours since lunch, and I had little hope in my ability to find anything remotely edible in the wild.

But just as I was getting ready to give up and seek shelter for the night (and I would have been asleep in minutes, my body exhausted from a full day's worth of hiking), the stream took a sharp bend to the left, the undergrowth suddenly cleared, and there, before me, I saw a man.

He was squatting down on a huge, flat rock that jutted out into the stream, his back to me, his head bobbing slowly up and down.

At that moment I realized that the constant hum and whir of the forest—the buzz of the insects, the chatter of the animals, the crackle of the leaves and brush underfoot—had somehow stopped. And the only noise I was hearing came from the man before me, a kind of repetitive chanting. Though I strained, I could not make out a word of what the man was saying, nor could I tell whether he was even speaking English.

I watched for a moment, unsure whether to interrupt what he was doing or continue lurking. He shifted position now, so that I saw him in profile.

I was too far away to see his face, but I could see now that he had long hair, almost down to his shoulders (and remember, this was 1939, a time when long hair on men was virtually unknown), a full beard, and something—a pouch, or a purse of some sort— hanging from a cord around his neck.

He reached down into that pouch now and pulled something out. A handful of sticks, I saw, with some string wrapped around them. He took the sticks and the string and began tying—or untying, I couldn't tell which at this distance—them together.

When he finished, he leaned over the rock and threw them into the water.

Just then, a shadow passed across the rock—a bird of some kind flying over, I couldn't quite tell from where. The man started.

His sudden movement, after such a long period of inactivity, startled me as well. I took a step backward.

Behind me, something growled.

I turned. The biggest German shepherd I'd ever seen in my life was a foot away, staring directly at me.

I like dogs, I really do. But this one looked ready to make a meal out of me.

Then it barked once and took a step toward me.

"Easy, Ranger."

I turned my head again, gradually this time (I did not want the dog to misinterpret any movement I made), and saw the man making his way down from the rock.

"Don't worry, Ranger's bark is worse than his bite," the man said as he reached us. "Especially if he thinks I'm in trouble."

"Believe me," I said, "I'm no trouble."

"Well, then. That's good." He held out his hand and smiled at me. "I'm Rustin. Rustin Parr."

High on the list of questions all the newspaper reporters and book writers and television people always wanted to ask me was if I could tell Parr was a killer when I met him. I never answered a one of them, not until I spoke to that Carrazco fellow, and even then, I couldn't bring myself to tell the whole truth about Rustin.

And I out-and-out lied to him about the Brody family.

But I think I'm getting ahead of myself.

I will say this now about Rustin Parr; from the very moment we shook hands, I knew I had nothing to fear from him. He had a simple, guileless manner, a ready smile, and such an obvious affection for his dog that I instinctively liked him.

A few days after the incident in the woods, when I told Burt Atkins about meeting Parr (when, in fact, I walked into the general store to finally buy that canteen), he asked me how Rustin

Graveyard in Maryland

was doing. They hadn't seen him around town for so long, he explained, that people were afraid he might have died.

I was in a good mood that day, which is why I didn't ask Burt the question which immediately popped into my head: Why hadn't anyone simply gone out into the woods to check how he was? Instead, I told him that Rustin seemed fine.

"Good." He smiled. "I worry about that boy sometimes."

Atkins's attitude toward Parr, I found out, pretty much mirrored the entire town's; they didn't like him hanging around, but at the same time they wanted to make sure he was all right. I heard a rumor that the Parr family had once been important in Burkittsville, which might have explained that.

Whoever and however important his kin had been in town, Parr and the people of Burkittsville interacted hardly at all. It wasn't that he was retarded, or stupid, or bad-tempered (accusations which all made their way into the press over the years); he just didn't see much sense in a lot of the rules society expected people to abide by. Society, in turn, wanted nothing to do with him.

The people of Burkittsville, of course, did find a use for Parr later.

Scapegoat.

"You like to fish, Mr. Cazale?" Parr asked. He picked up a flat stone from the ground and threw it sidearm into the water, where it sank.

I shook my head. "Never done it, not even once."

"Really? That's what most people come out here to do." He found another flat stone and threw it. This one skipped twice before sinking. "So what brings you out to this part of the woods?"

"Well, to be quite honest, I'm lost."

"Well that explains it, I guess."

The dog barked.

"All right, boy, all right." Parr walked past me and ruffled the fur on the dog's head. "We'll get going. He wants dinner. That dog is spoiled rotten. Eats twice a day, and canned dog food. What do you think about that? A whole forest full of food, and he likes the canned stuff best. Takes all kinds, I guess."

He looked to me. "Are you hungry as well, Mr. Cazale? Would you like to come back home and eat with us?"

I smiled. "That's the best offer I've had all day, Mr. Parr."

"Good. Follow me, then."

As he turned, the pouch I'd glimpsed earlier swung out from behind his back, where it had been dangling, and I got my first good look at it.

It was made from an animal's paw: the claws—several inches long—were still attached. They looked sharp, they looked dangerous. Whatever kind of animal the paw had once belonged to—a bear, or a wolf, or some other large animal—would have been a formidable opponent.

"What do you do, Mr. Cazale?" Parr called over his shoulder. He was leading us straight into the heart of the underbrush at a brisk walk: a man, clearly, who didn't need blue paint to find his way through the forest.

"Actually, it's Father Cazale. I'm a priest."

"You don't say. A priest."

"That's right. What about yourself, Mr. Parr? What do you do?"

"Oh, whatever it takes, you know. Some odd jobs in town to make some money, a little gardening, do a little fishing down in the creek. Watch out here," he said as we passed through a particularly thick part of the brush. "These branches got thorns on 'em: they'll snap back and take your eye out."

"Thanks."

"You coming from the Burkittsville side of the forest?"

"Yes."

"I used to live in Burkittsville myself, but"—he shook his head—"got a little tired of being around so many people. And they all got cars, and radios now—what an awful racket."

I wondered what Rustin Parr would make of downtown Baltimore on a Friday night.

"So I came out to the forest. Been here for a few years now, gotten to know my way around."

"It's beautiful out here."

"Oh, yes, sir. But it can be a little dangerous at times. Me and

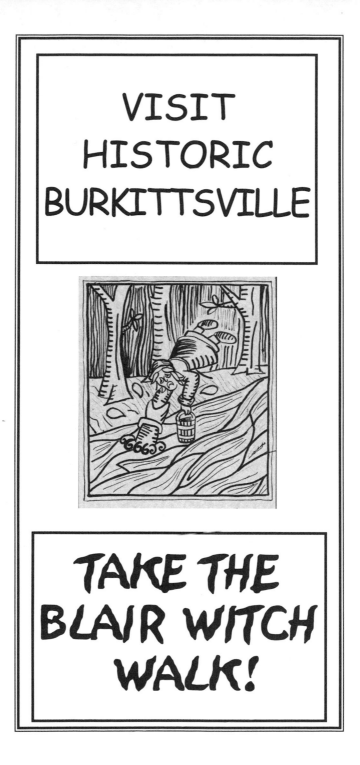

Ranger here"—and suddenly I saw the dog at his side again: it must have been trotting along silently the whole time—"we keep an eye on things."

The last few minutes we'd been on a steady climb upward. Now Parr pointed ahead of us, to the top of the rise.

"There's my house." He looked down. "You want some food, fella?"

Ranger barked once and took off like a bullet.

Parr laughed. "That dog loves to eat."

After dinner, Parr led me back to Black Rock Road and my car. He had no trouble finding it, even in the dark. I felt stupid when we got there: it only took forty-five minutes to walk from his house. I must have gone in a huge circle for a good portion of the day.

I can't remember much about that meal, or what Parr and I talked about through dinner. I do remember the house, though. Parr told me he'd done a great deal of the work on it himself. I told him he could be making a good living as a carpenter.

But when I think of that place in the woods now, I don't see it as it was that night. I see it as a ruin, a hole in the ground, with nothing left to it anymore save the stones of the foundation. The way Mary and I saw it last month, when after so many years I finally went back to Burkittsville to make my peace with the past.

The past, though, wasn't through with me just yet.

The next morning, when we woke up in the Holiday Inn in Frederick, Mary was already at the kitchen table, with the sleeve of her sweater rolled up.

"I must have brushed against poison ivy, or sumac, or something like that," she said. "Look at this rash."

June 7

4:00 A.M.

More and more, I have trouble sleeping. It's not just Mary, it's the weight of my entire life, crashing in on me. I suppose that's why I'm writing this journal now: to try and make sense of it all. Or

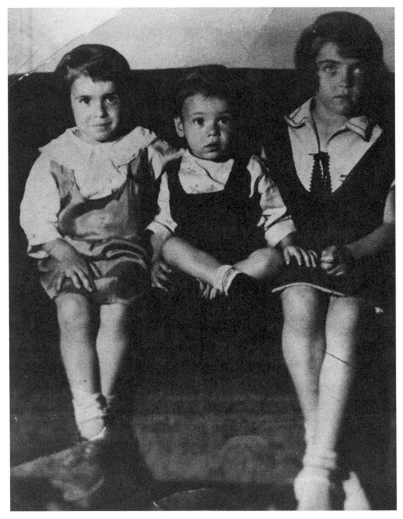

Julie Forsyth

perhaps that's not for me to do: perhaps it's for you who are
reading this to understand all that has happened to me.
As my father once said: the wheel will turn.
Does that make any sense?

10:00 A.M.

Mary seems to be living in her bed: it's all she can do to get up
and go to the bathroom. She has fallen into a state of apathy
about her condition, no longer amused at being the Illustrated
Woman, as she once called herself, whose fate is writ large on her
skin.
I, on the other hand, seem to be living in the past.
It is March of 1940. Monsignor Fannon has granted me a
week's leave from the parish to go back to Baltimore, where my
brother Joe is dying.

Vince, the eldest of us, always knew he was going to be an
actor. I, in the middle, was destined (at least according to my
mother) to become a priest.
And Joe, the baby of the family?
He tried out a number of different vocations: in March of
1940, he was a patrolman working the nastiest part of downtown
Baltimore when he walked in on a liquor-store holdup.
He killed both of the would-be robbers, but one of them got off
a shot as he went down that perforated Joe's stomach. Despite the
doctors' best efforts, infection set in. By the time I arrived at the
hospital, Joe was in critical condition with a raging fever. They
were sure he wasn't going to last the night.
I found my mother and Kathleen Shaughnessy (who Joe
always used to say was the girl he should have married) sitting in
chairs at the waiting room in St. Vincent's, bawling their eyes out.
When she saw me, my mother jumped up and hugged me so
tight I felt the vertebrae in my back crack.
"Easy, Ma." I wrapped my arms around her. "How is he?"
"Not good, Dom. I'm so glad you're here."
"Where's Vince?"

Kathleen stepped forward now and spoke. "He's on tour with a theater company in Canada. We haven't been able to reach him yet."

"Dom," my mother said, "you remember Kathleen Shaughnessy?"

"Sure. How are you, Kathleen?"

You're going to think ill of me for the next part.

Kathleen Shaugnessy (Mary Kathleen Shaughnessy, if you want her full name) and I had a bit of history.

Not much: she was a couple years younger than me while we were growing up, and it wasn't until I was in my last year of high school, when I already knew I was going off to seminary, that I first noticed her. At, of all things, a Knights of Columbus dance.

I should break off here to say it's a mistake to think that priests don't think of sex, or that they've somehow found a way to eliminate the urge from their systems. It's just that they have assigned it a lower priority in their lives, knowing that the pleasures of the flesh pale in intensity next to the fulfillment they are promised when they reach the kingdom of God.

Still, at times, your priorities do slip.

When mine did, they had a habit of wandering back to that K of C dance, and to a couple of dances Kathleen Shaughnessy and I shared. Bing Crosby was what I suppose you could call a teen idol back then, and his big song at the time was "Please." Not a slow dance, but not a fast one either—it called for the two of us to lay hands on each other, and I recall leading Kathleen nervously around the floor, sweating profusely the entire time. A decade after the fact, I still couldn't listen to any of Bing's songs, or watch his movies, without thinking of her.

As I said, you're going to think ill of me, but looking at Kathleen as she stood there in the hospital waiting room, her dark hair cascading off her shoulders, the soft skin at the hollow of her throat, I could hear Der Bingle sing again.

Thankfully, that moment passed—as did Joe's time in the hospital. He made a remarkable recovery, so much so that two days after I arrived, he was back on the ward and making jokes

with me about putting in a good word for the Senators with
the man upstairs. I knew it was safe to leave then and said my
good-byes to him and Kathleen, who as I recall was wearing a
flowered summer frock that, for the time, was very low cut.

It could have been my imagination, but my mother seemed in
an awful hurry to get me off of that ward.

The point being that when I climbed back aboard the bus
bound for Frederick, I was a little more preoccupied than usual
with the female of the species.

The attractive, dark-haired lady who took the seat across from
me didn't help things either. She had on a gray skirt that came to
just below her knee; as she reached up and placed her suitcase
into the overhead luggage rack, the skirt rose up her leg just a
little higher.

She had very nice legs.

I opened my newspaper and turned to the sports section.

The Yankees were still supposedly being sold to Jim Farley and
Jesse Jones: Joe D.'s brother Vince had been traded to Pittsburgh,
and Hank Greenberg was starting to clobber the ball at an
unbelievable pace.

It was a full news day elsewhere in the paper as well, which
kept me occupied for much of the ride.

At times, however, I snuck a glance at the woman across the
aisle out of the corner of my eye. Still, I didn't even realize that's
when the bus pulled out of Bartonsville, heading toward Frederick,
the last stop on the line, that we were the only two passengers left
on board.

Until she turned to me and said, "You must be Father Cazale."

"I must be," was all I could think of to say. I hadn't intended to
be funny, but it was nice to see her smile. She had a nice smile.

She laughed. "Burt Atkins said you had a sense of humor."

"Let me guess: you're from Burkittsville."

She nodded. "I am. And I'm sorry we haven't had a chance to
meet until now. I've heard so much about you." She held out a
hand. "Caroline Brody. My friends call me Carol."

I am ashamed—and a little abashed—to admit that virtually
all the Latin I learned in seminary has gone to the great memory

The shelly farm

graveyard in the sky, I still remember every little detail about that bus ride with Caroline Brody.

The blouse she wore (white, with red bands around the neck and wrists), her hairstyle (a Jean Arthur–inspired bob), and above all, the excitement in her voice as she talked about her week at the twenty-fifth annual Baltimore tulip show, where she'd won an award for something called a yellow "moonlight" tulip.

"A certificate of recognition," she said. "Which is not the same as a ribbon, but still . . ."

"It's wonderful. Congratulations."

"Thank you. My husband thinks I spend too much time in the garden, so it will be nice to show him the payoff for all that hard work."

As we talked, I learned more about the tulip: it had a four-inch bulb and was, in her opinion, inferior to the one she'd entered last year, which had received no award from the judges. I learned more about Carol: she'd inherited her passion for gardening from her mother, she and Michael had been high school sweethearts, they'd once shared their house with Michael's brothers, until the mining accident.

Talk of brothers led to discussion of my own family, and what had brought me to Baltimore, which brought us around to the benefits of growing up in the big city versus growing up in the country. She was looking forward to raising her children in Burkittsville.

"Michael wants us to move to Pittsburgh, though," she said. "He's got a friend who's assistant manager at a foundry up there. If the job comes through, it'd be a lot more money for us." She shook her head then. "But I don't want to leave Burkittsville; we've got a lot of friends there. And I don't want to uproot Kyle just now—he's had a hard year at school."

"Does Michael know how you feel?"

"Yes. But he says we'll make friends in Pittsburgh easily enough—all of us." She sighed. "I know it's hard for him here: every day he spends in the mine, every time he walks down the street, he sees another memory. It's not good," she said in a voice grown suddenly distant, and it was almost as if she were talking to herself, rather than confiding in me. "It's not good at all."

I wondered, exactly, what wasn't good. But I didn't want to press the point: so I changed the subject. "Tell me about your daughter."

Carol's face lit up.

We were deep into a discussion on the difference between boy and girl babies—her sister in-law had a little boy about the same age as Carol's Janine, which was where her little girl had been staying while she was away—when we pulled into the station at Frederick. I helped Carol get her suitcase down from the overhead rack and walked her to the parking lot outside the station.

"I can give you a ride back to Burkittsville, if you like," I told her. "I'm going back to the parish to pick up Monsignor Fannon's car."

"That's nice of you, Father. But Michael is picking me up here." As she spoke, she scanned the parking lot. "I'm sure he'll be along shortly."

But when I drove past a couple hours later, she was still sitting on a bench out in front of the station.

"What happened to your husband?" I asked.

Her arms were folded across her chest. She looked angry.

"I'm sure I don't know," she said in a way that made me think she knew exactly where he was. "Is your offer of a ride still good?"

"Of course." I got out and opened the door for her, because in those days it was the kind of thing a man did for a woman, even if the man was a priest and the woman married. At least, I thought so.

Carol Brody looked a little surprised at the gesture—but as I shut the door behind her, I caught a glimpse of her smiling. As I said before . . . it was a nice smile.

We continued talking in the same vein as before, all the way into Burkittsville and down First Street right up to the front door of her house.

The porch light was on.

Kyle Brody was sitting on the steps, his arm (it looked like, at first glance) wrapped around a big German shepherd.

Next to him, with a wooden cigar box on his lap, sat Rustin Parr.

chapter twelve

Parr rose to his feet to greet us as we climbed out of the car. "Father. And you must be Mrs. Brody."

Carol wasn't having any small talk. "What on earth is going on here?" she asked, stepping in front of me. "Who are you? What are you doing with my boy? Kyle?"

Kyle looked up at the sound of his mother's voice.

"Ma!" he cried out. "Ma, help me!"

I hadn't seen the boy in several months. He'd gone through a major growth spurt in that time, crossing over that indefinable line that separates little boys from young men, a little early perhaps, but given the size of his father, that was understandable.

You could see the change in his face, which, even through the dirt-stained tear tracks that covered it, was thinner, with a new angle and shape to it; in the breadth of his shoulders; and in the length of his arms. But most of all, you could see it in his eyes. When we'd first met, traces of a child's curiosity were still in them. Now, those traces were gone, replaced by something a little colder, more calculating.

But perhaps, knowing what was to come as I do, I am being a little unfair, projecting too much on the little boy who sat there on the porch steps without moving, crying for his mother.

"Kyle!" Carol called again. "What is it?"

The boy still didn't move. In a second, I saw why.

Parr's dog had hold of Kyle's shirtsleeve in his mouth.

Carol saw it at the same time I did. "Oh my Lord," she said. "That dog—"

Parr made a clucking noise with his teeth; a split second later Ranger let go of the boy's sleeve.

Kyle ran to his mother's arms. "He bit me. The dog bit me!"

"He didn't bite you," Parr said. "He bit your shirt. And that was only to keep you from running away again."

I stepped forward now. "What's going on here?" I said quietly.

"I got to show this to the boy's father," Parr said quietly. He held up the wooden box.

"He's not home?" Carol asked. She turned to Kyle. "Where's your father gone, Kyle? Do you know?"

Kyle shrugged, wiping away his tears. "He said he was going to Frederick, to pick you up at the bus station."

"He wasn't there. Never mind." I could hear the anger in Carol's voice. She turned to Parr. "What is it you want, sir?"

"Like I said, ma'am, I want to show this to your husband. I want to show him what your son was doing in the woods."

"Ma, that man's lying, whatever he says is just a stinkin' lie." Kyle set his lips in a pout.

"Hush, Kyle. Didn't you hear what I just said, sir? My husband's not home. If it's got something to do with my son, you can show it to me."

"No, ma'am." Parr sounded definite. "I can't do that. I'll wait to see Mr. Brody."

"Perhaps you can show this thing to me, whatever it is," I offered.

Parr shook his head. "No, Father. It's not for your eyes either. I'll just wait, Mrs. Brody, if it's all right with you." He sat down again on the porch steps.

"It is not all right with me," Carol said. "I want you off my property. You've frightened my son half to death!"

"All right." Parr nodded and stood back up. He walked to the edge of the Brody's yard, Ranger following a step behind, and sat right down on the road.

Carol glared at him. Then, without taking her eyes off Parr, she said to me in a voice loud enough that Parr couldn't miss it, "Father, would you please run over to Town Hall and get the sheriff?"

"Already tried that, ma'am," Parr called back. "No one's there."

We stood locked in place for a moment. I was going to suggest that Rustin come back to the motel with me and wait for Brody there, when I heard a car approaching down Main Street. It turned onto First and a second later, it pulled into the Brodys' drive.

Michael Brody climbed out, slamming the door behind him. "What's going on here?"

He was walking a little clumsily, and a second later, I realized why. He was drunk.

"We're waiting for you," Carol said. "I came home and found this man"—she pointed to Parr—"sitting on our porch with Kyle, who's apparently done something this man will only talk to you about."

"Ma—" Kyle said.

"Hush," Carol told him, and that's when it dawned on me that in the entire time since we'd arrived, Carol had not even once asked her son about what he had supposedly done. I wonder now if she didn't already have a good idea of what it was.

Michael turned and noticed Parr for the first time.

"Who the hell are you?"

"Michael!" Carol said. "Watch your language. Father Cazale's here."

"He's heard the word before, haven't you, Father?" Not waiting for an answer, Michael turned back to his wife. "And where the *hell* were you? I waited at that bus station half the night."

And at a bar the other half, I had no doubt.

"We'll talk about it later," Carol said.

"Excuse me," Parr said. "Mr. Brody, I found your boy in the woods earlier today. I want to show you what he was doing, and then I'll be on my way."

"Show me?" Michael asked. "Why don't you—oh, no."

He turned to his son, and I saw the boy visibly shrink back into his mother's arms.

"So help me God, boy, I'll beat you within an inch of your life if you've done it again."

Michael's lips were set in a thin line. He seemed, all at once, to have sobered up.

"Let me see that box," he said to Parr, holding out his hand.

Parr gave it him.

Michael held it a moment, as if summoning up the courage to face what was inside.

I wondered just what it was that Kyle had done before.

Then Brody flipped the box open.

Whatever he saw drained all the color from his face.

From where I stood, all I could see was the inside of the lid, which was covered with red stains.

Brody handed the box back to Parr without a word.

"I'm sorry to have to show you that, sir," said Parr. "I'm even sorrier for those poor animals."

But Brody wasn't listening. He had already turned away and was walking toward his wife and son.

The boy made a whimpering noise and clung tighter to his mother.

"Michael, no." Carol put herself between Kyle and his father, who strode past me now, walking quicker, his anger visibly growing with every step.

"Mr. Brody, don't," I said, laying a hand on his shoulder. He pushed it off.

His face was no longer pale, but red with rage. That color, next to the darker skin on his face and neck where he'd been burned, made him look something other than human, a colossus come to vengeful life.

He brushed Carol aside as if she were a little girl, grabbed hold of Kyle with one arm, and with the other slapped him hard across the face.

"Damn you, boy!" Brody slapped Kyle again. "What the hell's gotten into you?"

Kyle said nothing in response; neither did he whimper or cry out. All traces of the little boy who'd clung to his mother a moment ago were gone: he just stood there and took it, like a man, as his father reached back and slapped him again and again.

I was struck once more by how big the boy had grown; in just a very few years, it was clear to me, Kyle Brody wasn't going to simply stand there and take the punishment his father dished out. He was going to give back as good as he got.

"That's enough, Michael," Carol said, her voice surprisingly calm. "Stop it."

"It's all right, Ma," Kyle said, staring at his father. "It don't hurt."

Which was exactly the wrong thing to say: Michael Brody drew his arm back and backhanded his son full force across the face.

Kyle flew in the air and landed on the ground.

Carol stared at her husband, shock etched on her face. "I said that was enough." She went to Kyle's side and bent over him.

"Leave me alone, Ma," he said, sniffling. Blood was running out of the corner of his mouth; he wiped it away with the back of one hand. "I'm all right."

"Kyle, let me—"

"Leave me alone!" he said, his voice quivering.

Carol stood up.

Michael Brody walked into the house and slammed the door behind him.

"Carol," I began, "can I do something to—"

"Please leave, Father," she said. "Both of you, please leave us alone."

Parr did as she asked, walking off toward the woods without another word, Ranger trotting along a step behind.

Kyle got up slowly from the ground, anger oozing from his every pore. It traveled along his gaze and finally came to rest on Rustin Parr's retreating back.

Then Kyle turned it on me. "We don't need you around here either, Father."

The way he said it, it sounded like a warning.

June 9

2:00 A.M.

Tonight at about eleven, I was reading in bed when Mary screamed and sat bolt upright in bed next to me.

"Oh, Dom." Her eyes were wide with fright. "I had the dream again."

"About Connie."

She nodded. I set down my book.

"Only it wasn't quite the same, this time. I was swimming with her, but somehow I was under the water, looking at her from underneath." Tears began running down Mary's cheeks. "The sunlight from above was shining down on her, framing her face. She was so beautiful, Dom. So beautiful."

"Don't do this, Mary."

She paid me no mind. "I wanted Connie to be with me. It's only fair, isn't it? We never got to be with each other for even one day. So I brought her to me, Dom. I brought her down under the water to be with me."

I fluffed the pillows underneath Mary's head and pulled the blanket up over her. "Shhh. Try and go back to sleep—"

"No!" She reached up and wrapped her arms around my waist, clinging to me like a child. "I don't want to sleep anymore, Dom."

June 14

8:00 A.M.

At five-thirty this morning, an epidemic of dog barking swept through my neighborhood.

I got up from bed (Mary, thankfully, remained fast asleep) and peeked through the blinds on the front window.

It was just past dawn: a woman was jogging past. She was in her late fifties, early sixties, I would say, and moving at a speed somewhere between a brisk walk and a jog.

The cause of all the barking? The dog trotting at her side, a big German shepherd with metal tags dangling off his collar. The noise

Eric Norris

of the tags clinking together apparently offended every other dog within hearing distance—although they didn't seem to bother the shepherd as he trotted effortlessly along at his master's side, turning his head first left and then right as they moved down the street. Keeping watch.

It was a few Sundays after the incident with Rustin Parr that I first held mass at the Brody household. Close to two dozen of us squeezed into the big front parlor downstairs. Carol had set a fine silk tablecloth over their dining table, and we used that as the altar.

I gave a sermon about good and evil, and the responsibilities men faced to confront the demons besieging their world. This was the spring of 1940: you'll remember, I trust, what was happening in Europe.

Anticipating a large crowd, I'd consecrated more hosts than usual. When mass was finished, I placed the consecrated Eucharist in a pyx on the altar, snapped it shut, and left the candles burning to announce the presence of Christ.

Then I went onto the front porch, where all the parishioners had gathered and were drinking tall glasses of lemonade Carol had set out on a table. I took a glass too. We'd started mass deliberately early that Sunday, knowing that the temperature was supposed to get close to ninety degrees that day.

Carol was leaning on the porch rail, deeply engrossed in a conversation with Katie Flynn. I joined them.

"I won't do it, and I won't let John do it either," Katie was saying. "I've heard enough of those stories."

Carol laughed. "Oh, Katie, you can't be serious. We go up there all the time. It's a beautiful place for a picnic."

Katie shook her head. "I won't let the twins near it."

"Near what place?"

"Oh, hello, Father," Carol said. "I thought that was a wonderful sermon."

"Well, thank you. But, please—don't let me interrupt. You two were talking about . . ."

"The witch," Katie said.

"Excuse me?"

"The Blair Witch. Elly Kedward."

I shook my head. "I'm afraid you've lost me."

Katie frowned. "You mean to say that you've been here for —
how long now?"

"A year and a half, almost."

"A year and a half, and you haven't heard any stories about the
witch?"

I had to admit that was true.

"Katie, maybe this isn't the time or place," Carol began.

"No, it's all right," I said.

Except it wasn't, not really: I have already mentioned the
Church's attitude toward such things. And yes, this was a private
home, but we had also just finished celebrating mass here not ten
minutes earlier; the juxtaposition was, at best, tasteless.

But I wanted the conversation to continue. It didn't have to be
about the witch, actually.

It just had to be with Carol.

I had seen her several more times, off and on, during the last
couple weeks, as we made plans to celebrate today's mass, but
never for more than a few minutes at a time. Quick, clipped
discussions, colored by the memory of what had happened the
night I'd driven her back from Frederick. Michael was there more
than once as well; I wanted to talk with her in private, the way we
had on the bus.

You may be thinking I wanted more than that.

Not so, not on that day, at least. What I wanted was
conversation and camaraderie. I know, I was supposed to be
getting that from the Church, and even more so, from my
relationship with the Lord, but to be honest, I think by that spring
of 1940, part of me already knew I was in the wrong business.
That, in following my mother's wishes for me, in trying to be the
good man that, at that time, I thought my father hadn't been, I
had ignored my own true calling.

So I finally learned a little about the local folklore, and then
Katie's husband, John, joined us, and we talked about the move
they were planning in the New Year. And the Flynns left, and

Albert Collins wandered down from the inn, and the talk turned to baseball, and I started explaining to Carol why the fact that Joe DiMaggio never struck out was one of the reasons he was such a good ballplayer, which led us into a discussion of the hit-and-run, and the importance of sliding hard into second, and positioning your infielders, and so on.

"Why, Father," Carol said to me at one point, smiling. "You should have been a teacher."

At which I laughed and happened to look around the porch.

Kyle was standing in the doorway, staring at me.

Shortly thereafter, I went back into the front parlor to collect the instruments of the mass.

The candles were out.

The pyx was open.

And the consecrated hosts were gone.

Someone must have cleaned them up by mistake, is what I told myself.

chapter thirteen

June 16
1:00 P.M.

When I was growing up in Woodbury, there was a boy in our neighborhood named Tim Kilroy. He lived just around the corner from us, but we never played together. Tim kept to himself: he'd be inside reading while the rest of us were out playing ball.

One day the two of us ended up walking home from school together. I asked him if he wanted to go down to the ball field and have a catch.

"Can't. Got something I have to do."

"What?"

He shook his head. "Can't tell you."

"Yeah, right. Come on—you're just gonna go sit inside and read. Come out and have some fun, for once."

"Can't. I really do have something to do."

"What?"

He studied me a moment. "You have to promise not to tell anyone."

"Okay. I promise."

"All right." Then Tim smiled, which I think was about the first time I ever saw him do that. "Come on."

He lived in a row house a few blocks from ours. I followed him down into the basement till we came to a padlocked wooden door.

Tim turned around and looked at me. "You promise, right?"

"Yeah, I promise." I was more than a little curious by now and gave little thought to what he was asking.

Tim took out a pocketknife and used the blade to pry off the hasp from the wall. The screws must have been loose already because it popped right out and into his hand.

"This used to be a stop on the Underground Railroad," he said. "There's all these tunnels back here. My parents don't like me going in them, through, 'cause they think it's not safe."

Tim reached for the knob and turned it.

The door swung open.

A blast of cool, damp air greeted us. It smelled of earth and mold and something else that I couldn't quite put my finger on.

Tim flicked the light switch on the wall; a single bulb lit up. "Neat, huh?"

"Neat," I said, not really sure, in fact, that I did like it. I much preferred sunlight to being underground in the dimly lit room before us.

Tim reached into his knapsack and pulled out a flashlight. "I have to check the traps. But let me show you."

He swung the light onto the far wall.

Nailed in neat little rows a dozen long were an array of mouse heads.

"What do you think?"

I had made Tim a promise, but in talking to Father Carew during my next confession (and back then, we did it in the little booths you see in the movies, not the way it is now, where you have to sit face-to-face with your priest and tell him what you've done—not conducive to baring the soul, in my opinion), what I had seen inevitably slipped out.

After that confession, I went and told Tim Kilroy's mother. Her reaction was much the same as Michael Brody's would be some ten years later in Burkittsville. Tim had trouble sitting down in school for a couple of days afterward and never ever confided in me again.

And I never got to ask him the question that had been on my mind since I first saw what was on that basement wall: Why? What made you do such a thing? Or, as Michael Brody put it, What the hell's gotten into you, boy?

The Church has an answer to that question: It is the devil who sits at our ear, urging us on to commit those wicked deeds. It is the devil who leads us down the garden path, as it were, and shows us the red, shining apple on the tree of knowledge.

It is the devil who shows us to the door beyond which evil lies. Man must open that door himself.

June 17

9:00 A.M.

One of my favorite pictures of Mary was taken at our wedding reception in 1949, in Harrisburg, Pennsylvania. It's of Mary and her sister, Eileen. The two of them are embracing: Eileen's holding the bridal bouquet, which Mary has just thrown. The picture is usually stuck to the side of our refrigerator with a magnet.

When I woke this morning, Mary had cut it in half and placed the part with Eileen in a picture frame next to our bed.

"Remember Connie's wedding?" she asked me.

Mass at the Brody household became a regular event.

One Sunday, a few weeks after the one I've described above, I was helping Carol put her furniture back into place when there was a commotion at the front door. Suddenly a number of the parishioners who had just left the house came scrambling back in, slamming the door shut behind them.

John Flynn was carrying his wife, Katie, in his arms. He laid her down on the couch.

One sleeve of her dress was soaked through with blood.

"It bit me," she said. "Oh, dear Lord."

Her eyes rolled back in her head, and she passed out.

Emily Hollands

"Here," Carol said, stepping forward with a pair of scissors. She cut away the sleeve of the dress and examined the wound. "Not too deep. But we'd better get the doctor."

"What happened?" I asked.

Martin Richardson, a farmer I had only just met this morning, was at the Brodys' window, shaking his head.

"Damn thing's still out there. Some kinda crazy dog. Jumped up and bit Mrs. Flynn as we were walking down the street. Probably got rabies."

I walked to Richardson's side.

Rustin Parr's dog, Ranger, was pacing back and forth in front of the house.

"Where's Michael keep his gun, Carol?" John Flynn said. "Somebody's gonna have to go out and shoot that thing."

"Wait a minute." Everyone turned to me expectantly, but I didn't know what to say next. If there was a chance the dog was rabid, it had to be shot. If it was running around biting people, it had to be shot. But—

"Can't wait," John Flynn said. "It might take off on us and then we'd never know if it had rabies. Carol, tell me where that gun is."

I turned back to the window.

Rustin Parr was walking down the street toward the Brody house, holding a rifle at his side.

I ran out onto the front porch, Richardson was a step behind.

"Stay back, mister!" he yelled. "That thing's got rabies!"

"It's his dog," I said.

Richardson shook his head. "That ain't gonna matter a bit."

"Ranger," Parr called out. "What's gotten into you, boy? What's wrong?"

The dog growled at him.

"It's me, Ranger. It's just me." Parr approached to within ten feet of the dog. Then he lowered the rifle to his side, and held out his hand. "Come on, come see. It's me, Ranger. Come." He smiled. "Everything's all right, Ranger."

The dog cocked its head then, and looked at Parr. It began whimpering.

"It hurts, doesn't it? I know, boy, I know." Parr squatted down. "Come here."

For a second, it seemed like everything was going to be fine. I heard the creak of the Brodys' front door opening behind me, and the sound of footsteps on the porch.

Ranger snarled and leapt.

Parr moved, quicker than I would have thought possible, rolling to his side. He raised the rifle and fired: Ranger fell to the ground.

I was the first to reach them. Parr was kneeling next to his dog, gently smoothing the fur on his head. Ranger was lying on his side, eyes wide and unseeing, his belly exposed.

There were marks of some kind burned into his stomach: they almost looked like writing.

"I shouldn't have left him alone for so long," Rustin was saying. "It was my fault. I made a mistake. Somehow . . ." His voice trailed off and he looked at me. "Hello, Father."

"Hello, Rustin." I put a hand on his shoulder. "I'm so sorry about this."

I knelt down next to him. Parr seemed to have aged ten years.

Parr nodded. "I'm going to take him home now."

He bent down then and picked up Ranger in his arms.

"Hey, you got to leave the body!" That was Richardson, calling out. "We got to see if it's rabid."

Parr didn't even break stride.

"Hey, mister!"

I turned back to the Brody house.

Kyle sat on the steps, next to his mother. "I knew that was a bad dog, Mom," he said, looking up at her.

Two months later, I got John Flynn to show me the way to Parr's house. I wanted to see how Rustin was doing.

But when we got there, the place was deserted.

Vines had begun climbing up the front door.

"No one's been here for a long time," Flynn said.

June 18

10:00 A.M.

Yesterday, it was dogs barking that woke me.

Today, it was a cat.

I walked out into the kitchen and saw Mary chasing Socks, the Wards' Siamese, around the kitchen table. I didn't ask how she'd gotten it inside (I later found a package of catnip in the kitchen cupboard), or what she would have done had she caught it.

I led Mary back into the bedroom, then let the cat out the back.

When she was asleep, I went down to Kroger's and bought a lock for the bedroom door.

1:00 P.M.

I have been dreaming as well.

My dreams are of that day I went to the hospital to visit Joe, after he'd been shot. In those dreams, my baby brother doesn't recover from his wounds.

When Vince walks into the waiting room, he finds Ma and me and Kathleen, sobbing in each other's arms.

And then we have to go on living in that reality, where Joe is dead, for the rest of our lives, without waking up.

Another nightmare I never seem to wake up from: November 16, 1940, when I stepped through the doors of the Burkittsville Town Hall, and into the middle of a war council.

chapter fourteen

Around a hundred people lived in the town at
that time; every one of them, it seemed to me, had jammed into
the courtroom for this meeting.

Three men sat side by side at the judge's pulpit: Mayor Ron
Muller, Sheriff Damon Bowers, and Burt Atkins. Bowers's deputy,
Charlie Hobart, stood behind him, next to an American flag.

As I entered, Bowers stood and banged down a gavel. "Find
some seats, and let's get started."

There was scuffling and murmuring, and Albert Collins, who
was on his way out to the meeting as I was pulling into the inn,
led me over to what was the jury box, where extra rows of folding
chairs had been set out.

A little girl had been kidnapped a few days ago, he told me.
Nobody had any idea who'd done it, or why.

"Let me start by bringing you all up to speed," Mayor Muller
said. He was a thin man with spectacles, the start of a potbelly
and a receding hairline who I had met one morning at the
Flynns' house. A bachelor and a banker, he worked down in
Frederick and lived on the family farm, which his father and
brother ran. "We placed a call to the FBI, in the hopes of getting
some more people out in the woods. Maybe a little more
manpower on the investigation too."

Bowers's face tightened at this last remark.

"We have no real news at this point, I'm sorry to say. The sheriff's got three search parties going in the woods, which I'm going to let him tell you about in a minute, and Jack Flippy's got two teams of dogs out with them and a third coming in from Leaderville in the morning." Muller cleared his throat; he seemed slightly lost to me, a little bit dazed by the whole situation. "Anybody has any other ideas about what we could— or should—be doing, you can talk to the sheriff, who I'm going to turn this over to now. Damon?"

Muller sat, and Bowers stood. He had a pad of paper in his hands and immediately started reading from it.

"Here's what we know. Wednesday afternoon, sometime between four and five o'clock, Emily Hollands disappeared from her own backyard. Mrs. Hollands remembers Emily went outside right after the two of you finished listening to American Cavalcade on the radio together, is that right, Mrs. Hollands?"

The sheriff looked up from his paper toward the audience. Everyone's eyes went toward a man and a woman in the second row, his arm around her, her head on his shoulders. Carol Brody, I saw, was sitting next to the woman, holding her hand.

The woman nodded, and Bowers, having got his confirmation, continued reading.

"While Mrs. Hollands was in the kitchen, getting dinner ready, Emily was playing out in the backyard. When she called Emily in—five o'clock, to help get the food on the table—the child didn't answer. Mrs. Hollands went out to the backyard, where she found a hair ribbon Emily had been wearing, and—"

Mrs. Hollands started sobbing.

A man I didn't know stood up. "Is it necessary to put them through this all again? We know what happened."

The crowd murmured its assent.

Bowers looked surprised by the interruption.

"What we want to know," the man continued, "is what else we could be doing to—"

A sharp crack rang out.

I looked up—as did everyone else in the room—to see Burt

Atkins standing next to Bowers, holding the gavel. He looked angry, but when he spoke, his words were anything but.

"I know this is a painful time for all of you, and your hearts—like mine—go out to the Hollandses." The murmuring that had been going on ceased, people's backs straightened, and everyone leaned forward to listen.

"You give them all whatever help you can," Atkins continued. "But I want you to give the sheriff here your attention, and the benefit of your thinking. Whoever took this little girl, my guess is one of you out there saw him—maybe in town, out on the road somewhere, out in the woods around your farms. I want you to think real hard now—real hard. If you remember anyone like that, you tell Sheriff Bowers, or one of the deputies." Bowers nodded. "We'll catch who did this, and we'll find Emily, safe and sound. I have no doubt about it. Sheriff?"

Atkins handed the gavel to Bowers and sat.

The meeting went on without further interruption, and I learned that Bowers and his deputies had been combing the woods since the evening the child disappeared, with nothing to show for it. One of Flippy's dogs (Jack deFillippi was his real name, but everyone called him Flippy) had turned up a shoe that may or may not have belonged to Emily, but that was the only clue of any sort that had surfaced in the three days since the girl had gone missing.

Afterward, I joined the line of people offering sympathy to George and Elizabeth Hollands—and then, at my suggestion, right there in the courtroom, we prayed. Carol Brody and a few others prayed with us.

I helped the Hollandses as much as I could over the next few weeks, as hope of finding Emily faded, and despair set in. We read psalms and sought comfort in the words of Scripture even as their despair faded away into a kind of listless apathy.

Many nights, Carol Brody was with us.

And somehow, when those painful evenings were done, I would end up talking to Carol about things a little more pleasant: what she'd been doing in her garden, what her daughter had been up to. She got her hair cut one weekend in Frederick; I noticed,

Elizabeth Hollands's vigil

and that pleased her. There was more than one night when I would walk her home and head back to my room at the inn, thinking of her the same way I had thought of Kathleen Shaughnessy so many years before. It was wrong, it was foolish, and yet I couldn't stop.

Talking was all we were doing, and yet, all the same, it was as if the two of us were courting.

Michael Brody was almost never to be seen. From Gretchen, the waitress at the diner, I heard that he was working at one of the big West Virginia mines and spent several nights there a week.

Carol and I never talked about him. Or about Kyle, who would sometimes be waiting up when I walked his mother home. He was perfectly polite to me, but nothing more. No mention of push-button gearshifts, no mention of Rustin Parr or his dog.

One night Carol and I were particularly late coming back from the Hollandses. It was just a few days before Christmas, which I remember because Burt Atkins had put up the biggest Christmas tree I'd ever seen in the parking lot of the inn. He was doing his best, it seemed to me, to remind folks that despite what had happened, there were still some things worth celebrating.

We had yet to come to that tree. We were still walking down Main Street, Carol pushing Janine in the baby carriage in front of her, when she stopped and pointed to one of the older houses.

"Want to hear a story?" she asked.

"Does it have a happy ending?"

She shook her head. "It's a ghost story."

"Ah. Like the one about the witch you told me before." I shrugged. "All right. I'm game."

Carol smiled. "You know, Father—you are unlike any other priest I've met."

"How so?"

She hesitated a moment. "You seem more—oh, I don't know—inclined to talk with us, rather than just preach. Do you know what I mean?"

"I do. And I'm flattered."

"Oh, it's not just me, Father. We've all talked about it—a lot of people feel the same way."

"Well, thank you Carol." We had stopped walking, I suddenly realized, and were standing face to face with each other. "I like to think I'm a good listener."

"You are," she said simply.

I cleared my throat. "So tell me this ghost story."

We started walking again.

"Well," she said. "Burkittsville was a pretty important place during the Civil War, you know. Both armies—North and South—passed through here more than once. Now the family who lived in that house back there, they were Rebel sympathizers. So when this wounded Rebel soldier was too sick to move on with his company, they took him in."

We were at the inn now, with Burt Atkins's tree looming before us.

"But the Union Army showed up unexpectedly, so they had to hide him down in their basement. And then the Union forces pitched tents right on their front yard, and stayed for a few weeks."

"I can see this isn't going to have a happy ending."

She smiled. "Well, either the family forgot about the soldier in their basement, or they just couldn't get food to him—the story isn't completely clear. What happened for sure is that when the Union Army finally left, and the family went down into the basement to check on that soldier, all they found was a skeleton. And they say till this day, you can sometimes hear that soldier, howling at night for food."

"That's an awful story."

She looked at me, an expression of concern on her face. "I hope I didn't offend you, Father."

"Oh, no," I said quickly. "Took my mind off things for a moment, for which I thank you."

"Well then . . . you're welcome," she said.

"So what else should I know about this town?" I asked. "You seem to be the expert."

"My family has been here for a long time," she agreed.

Just then, we turned the corner and came to her house. I thought I saw a curtain fall back in place on one of the upstairs windows. Kyle? Or Michael? Or my imagination?

I thought then about stopping those impromptu sessions at the Hollandses, but didn't. I convinced myself that the "courtship" was all in my head: what we were doing was perfectly innocent. Carol, after all, never did anything to encourage me. But I must say, looking back on that time, she never discouraged me, either.

I was walking a tightrope: the slightest surprise, and I would stumble and fall.

And then Kyle disappeared.

I was at the church in Frederick, chaperoning a dance for the teenagers there, when Mrs. McCabe asked me to come take a phone call in the rectory.

It was Carol.

"Kyle's gone."

At first, I didn't understand. "Has he run off again?" He'd done that more than once, after fighting with his father. "Do you want me to go pick him up someplace?"

"No." Then she started crying. "That's not what I mean. He's gone. Kidnapped. Just like that other girl."

"Oh, dear God . . . no."

"Michael and the sheriff went out a little while ago with a group of men. Mrs. Bowers is going to stay here with me for a little while, but—"

"I'm on my way." And then, without even asking Monsignor Fannon's permission, I took the black Ford and set out for Burkittsville.

There was, to coin a phrase, hell to pay the next day.

But by then, I was long fallen from grace.

It was a miserable night for driving: freezing rain and sleet coming down, and the roads so slick that I could barely make twenty miles an hour on the winding mountain way.

I think it was on that drive, from Frederick to Burkittsville, that I realized I was never going to be a priest.

I should have been thinking about Kyle and Emily, praying for their safe return. Or Michael Brody and Damon Bowers, and the men who were with them, out in those woods in the middle of this storm, no doubt half-blinded by the falling rain, in the middle of their impossible search for any trace of those children and whatever madman had taken them.

But I wasn't thinking about any of those things. My mind had jumped ahead to the house on First Street, where Carol was waiting.

She opened the door, wearing a long white dress, cinched at the waist with a belt, her hair pulled back into a bun. A fire was blazing in the hearth behind her.

"Father, thank you for coming."

"Any news?" I asked, wiping my shoes on the mat.

"Mrs. Bowers just left. She's going up to Town Hall to see if they've heard anything. Those are soaked." Carol pointed to my shoes. "Take them off, and I'll put them by the fire."

"Thank you."

"Are you cold?" She put my shoes on the stone next to the hearth. "Let me get you some tea." She headed toward the kitchen.

"Don't go to any trouble, please," I called after her. "You should be resting."

"It's good for me to be doing things. It takes my mind off what's happening. It'll just be a minute."

The floor was cold against my bare feet. I walked to the front porch window and saw that, outside, the rain was changing into snow. Worse for driving in, easier to track footprints through—I guessed.

Upstairs, a child started to cry.

"Oh, that's Janine," Carol said, coming out of the kitchen with a cup of tea. "I'll be right back."

While she was gone, I sipped my tea. The strain of the drive had made me tired, I realized. The tea felt good going down; it relaxed me, warmed me from the inside out.

I stood next to the fire and warmed the outside of my body as well.

A few minutes later, Carol came back downstairs.

"She's asleep again." She smiled at me. "Thank you again for coming."

"Not at all." I set my tea down on the mantel above the fireplace. "Now tell me—when did this all happen?"

"Kyle's been gone for two days. At first, we thought maybe he had run away. There's a place in the woods he sometimes goes to. But when Michael went out in the morning to look . . . he wasn't there."

"Is there someplace else he might have gone?"

"No," she said, shaking her head. "Look at this weather— where else could he go?"

"Could he be lost?"

"No. He knows those woods. Something's happened to him, I know it." She came closer and stood next to me at the fire. "Katie Flynn says there are monsters out there; maybe it's true." Carol dabbed a handkerchief to the corner of her eyes. "Excuse me, Father."

I was suddenly aware of how close the two of us were standing. I smelled something on her then: perfume, a hint of lilacs.

I stepped back.

"Perhaps there is a psalm we can read," I said.

"If you like." She wiped another tear away and turned to face me. "Your readings are always a comfort to me."

Why do I remember this now?

Mary Kathleen Shaughnessy, standing next to me at Joe's funeral, tears running down her cheeks, both her hands clasping one of mine. Vince is singing "Amazing Grace"—but as Mary leans her head on my shoulder, it's Bing Crosby I hear:

"You have the soul of an angel white as snow . . . here I stand your reluctant Romeo . . ."

Tears ran down Carol Brody's cheeks.

My head was pounding. The warmth of the fire on my skin, the tea warming me from inside, the smell of lilacs, the sense of Carol standing right there within reach . . .

I opened my arms and drew her into them.

It seemed the most natural thing to do: a gesture of comfort between two human beings, an act completely innocent in intent.

Janine & Carol Brody

Or so I told myself.

In my embrace, her tears fell faster. She started sobbing, full-throated cries that shook her body and mine. She said things too: how her whole world was falling apart, how misunderstood Kyle was, how distant Michael had been to both her and their son, how much of a comfort our talks had been.

To be truthful, I missed a great deal of it. The whole world to me was her, in my arms.

And when the worst of her crying had subsided, and she pulled away from me, it again seemed natural—the human thing to do—to wipe away her tears with my fingers.

She looked up at me then, and said my Christian name.

And God help me, I was lost.

June 19

11:30 A.M.

I kept that night a secret for sixty years.

Now, it seems, I can't stop talking about it.

The morning we returned to Hallandale, after we had gone to Dr. Weitzmann, I sat down and told Mary everything. What had happened between Carol Brody and me the night Kyle disappeared—and what came afterward.

"Shhh," she said when I had finished. "That's all in the past, it doesn't matter anymore." But it does.

June 20

11:30 A.M.

The Church knows the importance of history.

The day before he was to leave on vacation, I called Father Callahan. Even the furniture in his office had been packed away by then, so we went outside and sat on a bench at the back of the church.

"I was glad to hear from you, Dominick," he said. "Now, what can I do for you and Mary?"

I lowered my head into my hands and began to cry.

"What is it Dom? What's wrong?"

I sniffed and wiped away my tears. "Bless me, Father, for I have sinned. It's been six weeks since my last confession."

"Easy now, Dom. Six weeks—it's not possible to have done something so terrible in that time."

"No," I said, gathering myself. "But what I have to confess goes back further."

"Tell me."

So I did—about Carol Brody, and what we did that night while I wore the uniform of a priest, while her husband searched in a raging storm for their first child, while her second slept blissfully upstairs next to their marriage bed.

All the rest, I told him too: about Rustin Parr, and what had happened in Burkittsville in 1941. Why I'd kept silent about Parr's last words all these years, why I had broken that silence, why I had gone back to Burkittsville.

He had the same reaction as Mary to that part: he didn't believe me either.

In fact, when I was done, he not only suggested penance, he suggested, ever so gently, that I might want to consider talking to someone other than a priest.

"Surely, Dom," he said when I finished, "you're imagining some of this."

chapter fifteen

Six months passed.

Six more children disappeared.

And then, in the spring of 1941, Burkittsville's long nightmare ended.

I was in my room at the inn, when I heard a shout from outside.

When I got downstairs, Burt Atkins was standing in the door to the street, holding it open.

"They got him," he said. "They got the sonuvabitch."

I shook my head. "Who?"

"The killer. The monster. The one who stole those children."

My blood turned to ice. "Killer?"

"They're dead." Tears began to run down Atkins's face. "All dead, buried in his basement, the butcher. He—"

Atkins fell to his knees. The door swung shut and slammed into his back.

He didn't seem to notice at all.

I should have stayed with him, to offer some words of comfort.

Instead, I left him slumped over, sobbing, and walked slowly down the road to the Brody house.

Carol and I had been virtual strangers since that night six months earlier. I remember slipping out of her house like a thief,

Yet another search party

walking slowly through the falling snow, letting the cold and wet soak through me, as if they could somehow wash me clean again. When I returned to the inn, I ran into Albert Collins at the desk. He told me there was no news on the Brody search.

"You look chilled to the bone, Father. You haven't been out there searching yourself, have you?"

I shook my head.

"I could start a fire down here, if you want. Warm you up a little."

I shook my head again and went upstairs to my room.

I was up all night, watching the snow fall.

The next day, I told Mrs. Sullivan we should hold Christmas mass at her farm: it was too difficult for the Brodys now, with what had happened to Kyle.

Carol did not show up that Sunday, or the next or the next.

Then, as more children vanished, the people of the town came together as one to worship. We held several interfaith prayer sessions in the town's sole church, with the Lutheran minister presiding. It was easy for me to get lost in the crowd there, to avoid her entirely.

One morning I passed her on the street: she was walking with Ingrid Thompson, whose own son Steven was to vanish shortly thereafter.

We stopped a moment to talk.

"How have you been, Father?" Carol asked. Her breath made steam in the air.

"Fine. And yourself?"

"I'm good. Best as can be expected under the circumstances. Michael's home now. And Janine is growing so fast . . ." Her voice trailed off.

"No news, I take it?"

She shook her head. "No news."

"You and Kyle are in my prayers."

We stood looking at each other a moment. I couldn't think of a single word to say.

So I turned to Mrs. Thompson and began talking with her.

That was the worst thing of all, that we no longer had anything to talk about. It was as if whatever force had drawn us together had dissipated, all its strength used up in achieving its desired goal.

Yet even so, with the news Burt Atkins had brought, I knew that I had to offer her some words of comfort.

When I got to the Brodys' house, the sheriff's car was parked in front. Charlie Hobart was leaning against it, tears running down his face.

He was smiling.

I didn't understand, till I looked at the front porch.

Where Michael and Carol Brody stood, hugging their son.

"He's alive," I said.

"He's the only one," Hobart said. "He escaped. He showed us where it happened."

"Father Cazale," Carol said, detaching herself from her husband and son. "Did you hear? They caught him. It's over."

"Who was it?" I asked.

"It was Parr, Father. It was Rustin Parr."

At the trial I barely recognized him.

Shooting Ranger may have aged him ten years, but the acts Parr stood accused of now had simply diminished him: he looked somehow deflated to me, like a circus balloon left lying on the ground after the show has packed up and moved on, emptied of the energy that had sustained it, void of hope, and life itself. His right forearm was wrapped in bandages: the wound, Charlie Hobart told me, was self-inflicted, though Albert Collins assured me in confidence that it was only the most visible of the bruises Parr had sustained at the hands of his captors.

Parr sat slumped down in his chair, rubbing that arm, throughout the entire course of the trial, a blank expression on his face.

Not that his appearance would have made a bit of difference, in the long run. From the moment he was accused, Rustin Parr was going to hang.

No lawyer in the county would stand up for him; they finally had to import an attorney from Baltimore to defend him, a man named Biester, who started the trial by raising objection after

Abbot Genser

Rustin Parr

objection and ended it slumped over in his chair, denied the
opportunity by the judge to present even a single witness on
Rustin's behalf.

And through it all, Rustin sat there hollow-eyed, never offering
a word in his defense. What could he say? There was the damn-
ing evidence in the basement, there were the children's things
scattered throughout the house, and there was Kyle Brody.

That little boy, standing up in court and giving graphically
detailed testimony about what Parr had done, sealed Rustin's fate,
more than any other single piece of evidence.

I can still see the look on Kyle's face as he told the jury how
Parr had brought him down to the basement at knifepoint, made
him stand facing the corner while he killed the other children.
That look scared me, more so even than the cruel calculation I'd
seen in his eyes the night I'd driven Carol back from the
Frederick bus station. That calculation, at least, was a sign of life.

His eyes now were dead. His voice, as he recounted the story of
his kidnapping and all the things that came after, was flat, void of
tone and emotion; an old man's voice. I wondered how badly the
boy had been damaged by what had happened to him.

The look on Carol's face scared me too. Not just the anger she
so visibly radiated at Parr, but the satisfaction on her face as Kyle
testified. Whenever her son's testimony faltered, he would look to
her, and she would tighten her lips and nod her head, as if willing
the boy to continue.

And Rustin, I didn't understand at all. I sent a message to him
through Charlie Hobart, asking if he wanted to talk. He never
responded.

He was convicted within a week and sent to the state prison in
Rockville to await execution.

June 21

Quick trials were a hallmark of the witch-hunts, as well.

The accusation in and of itself was proof of guilt; a confession
was then secured through torture. And if more evidence was
needed . . . the inquisitors would strip the victim naked and

search for the devil's mark. This was said to have been placed upon the witch by Satan himself, to mark him/her as an initiate into the black rites.

The mark could be anything, as far as the inquisitors were concerned. Any disfiguration at all was seen as inarguable proof that the accused had been consorting with the devil: a scar, a birthmark, a mole. . .

A burn, perhaps.

The months passed, and a semblance of normalcy returned to Burkittsville.

It was only a semblance, however.

Every child in town under the age of sixteen went nowhere alone; every stranger coming through town was directed immediately to Sheriff Bowers. Whole families packed up and moved away, some fleeing the memory of what had happened, others chased away by things far less tangible.

"It was that old woman—the witch—made him do it, that's what he told Damon," Ingrid Thompson said. A few of us were standing in front of the Thompsons' farm, where we'd just spent the afternoon helping Ingrid and her husband, John, load up their car and a trailer with all their worldly possessions.

They were taking their remaining child—their daughter Heather—to Minnesota, where John had family in the shipping business.

"It's as far away from Burkittsville—and those woods- as we can get," Ingrid said.

Some were less scared of the woods. It was one of those, I assume, who hiked into them and burned down Rustin Parr's house.

As for Parr himself . . .

Shortly after the trial, he'd been moved to the state penitentiary at Rockville after Bowers received word that a lynch mob was forming. Still, his name was on everyone's lips, as the day of the execution approached.

People were carpooling up to go to the prison and watch him swing.

The afternoon before his execution, I was in Frederick, talking with Monsignor Fannon about my role in the parish. He had begun to sense a waning of my enthusiasm for the job and had called me in to discuss it.

I almost told him about Carol Brody.

When I came out of his office, I found Charlie Hobart waiting for me with his car.

"It's Parr," Charlie said. "He wants to see you."

June 22

It all went wrong when we hiked into the woods.

Up until that point, my return to Burkittsville—apart from the nonstop chatter of our guide—had been a cathartic experience, far more so than my half-truthful interview with that filmmaker.

I felt foolish for skulking about back in town the way I had, hiding beneath my overcoat, even more foolish for all those years I'd spent running from my past, when the things that had haunted me for all those years turned out to be the products of my own overactive imagination.

Then Mary stepped over the foundation wall and stood on the ground where those seven children had been buried.

The air itself seemed to shimmer; for a moment, I thought I saw Rustin Parr's house standing there intact, looking exactly as it had the day John Flynn and I hiked into the woods. Front door open, vines climbing up the outside of the house . . .

The writing on the walls.

"What a tragedy," Mary said, hands on hips, surveying the ruins. She looked up at me. "Dom? What is it? What's wrong?"

I couldn't find my voice.

"Poor man," Mary said, crossing quickly to my side. She put a hand to my brow. "You're white as a sheet."

June 25

No more good days.

Mary sits in bed and scratches at her arm.

Mary curses at me in language so foul I cannot bear to repeat it, even here.

Then she collapses in tears, begging me to let her see Connie.

I gave her a Valium this morning, then bundled her into the car and drove around until 9:00 A.M. when I took her to the doctor down in Miami that I started seeing last Christmas. He asked her some questions and ran some tests.

He pulled me aside and suggested some facilities.

"I'm going to send a man in there with you," the warden at Rockville State Penitentiary—a man named Alvin Creeg, who looked to be as big around as he was tall—said. "In case he gets out of line." Creeg waved forward a guard who stood behind him. "Williams here. He'll keep the bastard under control, won't you, Ben?"

The big man smiled and removed his billy club from his equipment belt. "Whatever needs doing," he said, patting the palm of one hand with the club.

"That really won't be necessary, Warden," I said. "I know Rustin. He's not going to harm me."

Creeg shook his head. "He's a killer, Father. A crazy man. Been shouting all sorts of crazy things these last few days. Doc had to shoot him up a couple times to quiet him down. Even that didn't do it once, so we had to shove him back into line forcefully. You'll want Ben to go with you."

I shook my head. "I don't."

Creeg glared up at me. "It's your funeral." He looked up at Charlie Hobart, who'd driven me down to the prison and escorted me in. "You're a witness?"

"I'm a witness." Charlie turned to me. "You take care in there, Father. You may think you know this man, but he's gone round some kind of corner here. He's not what he was before he killed those kids."

I nodded. "I'll be careful."

Williams led me out of the warden's office and onto the cell block proper. Most of the inmates were outside, getting their exercise for the day: the prison was empty, and quiet. It felt as if

steven Thompson

the iron all around us, every bar and cage and lock we passed by, had been constructed for the sole purpose of keeping Rustin Parr safely tucked away from the rest of the human race. When we came at last to his cell, it all seemed totally unnecessary.

He sat on the bottom bunk, hands on his knees, staring at nothing at all.

"Here's your man," Williams said. "Now I'm gonna open this door and lock you in. Then I'm gonna walk off a little down the hall. You call for me when you want to get out, okay? And remember—be careful. He's a loon."

"I'll be careful."

"You be good, Parr," Williams said. " 'Less you want some more of this." The guard pulled his billy out and twirled it. "You hear me?"

Rustin nodded his head up and down slowly. I saw a big black-and-blue mark then, on the side of his face.

That was from Williams, I assumed, giving him some of "this."

"I'm not gonna do anything," Parr said.

"Good." Williams stepped back from the cell door and let me enter. "He's all yours, Father. You call if you need me."

"Thank you." I stepped into the cell, and Williams shut the door behind me. I waited till I heard his footsteps disappear down the corridor before speaking.

"Hello, Rustin."

He put one hand on the bunk and, as if every movement cost him inconceivable effort, twisted himself around so that we were squarely opposite each other.

Then he tilted his head back and looked up at me.

I stared into the eyes of madness.

"Bless me, Father," Parr said, "for I have sinned. It's been thirty years since my last confession."

chapter sixteen

Looking back over this journal, I realize there is something important I neglected to write down, which happened a few days before Rustin Parr walked into town to confess.

There was a string of forest fires up in the Black Hills, on the Hagerstown side of the forest, stretching down from Stone Quarry Ridge into the valley. Those fires, according to Burt Atkins, who owned a good chunk of land in the area, all appeared to have been of incendiary origin.

In other words, they were deliberately set.

June 27

I opened my eyes this morning to the sight of Mary standing at the bedroom door. At first, I thought she was trying to open it.

Then I saw what she had done.

All around the doorway, the wall was covered with symbols she had drawn in the night: runes, which matched those on her arm.

The symbols were red.

She'd used her own blood.

✳   ✳   ✳

"I want to confess," Parr repeated. "Hear my confession."

I shook my head. "Rustin, I can't—"

"I was baptized. Dale and me, down at St. Joseph's in Frederick." He pushed himself to his feet, his right forearm, I saw, was still bandaged, as it had been during the trial.

He began pacing around the cell.

"Everything all right down there?" the guard called.

"Everything's fine!" I called back. I turned to Parr, who was still pacing. "You want me to hear your confession, Rustin? Let me see if we can use the chapel."

"Don't need no chapel. Got to be here. Now."

I shook my head. "I don't—"

"Bless me, Father," Rustin began, seeming not to hear me at all. "It has been thirty years since my last confession."

Charlie Hobart was right: he'd gone round the bend.

I sighed. "Hold on. If we're going to do this, let's do it right."

Parr nodded. "Let's do it right."

And so we began.

Before too long, we came back to the words Parr had started with.

And then, for a moment, he was silent.

I waited for him to continue.

"Rustin?"

He rolled up the sleeve of his shirt then and ripped off the bandage.

June 28

Sometimes, I'm not sure of anything.

It all runs together in my head; the symbols on the walls of Rustin's house, the markings on Mary's arm, what Rustin showed me that evening in the prison . . .

The witch's cipher.

All those years, I imagined the past chasing me, calling after me in a language I could not speak. At times, I thought my fears groundless, the product of an overactive imagination, as Father Callahan said.

Now, I know better.

I know who, and what, they want.

And I know how to stop them from getting it.

Mary didn't believe me at first, even when I showed her the symbols in the book I'd taken out from the library.

"All this witch nonsense," she said. "Is this some kind of prank you're playing, to try and frighten me?"

June 29

I thought I was done with the story of Rustin Parr.

No matter. Let me finish writing it now, before Mary wakes up again.

The prison was alive with the sound of inmates all returning from their exercise period: boots on concrete, cell doors opening and shutting, voices laughing and talking.

A troop of prisoners walked past us: they looked in at Rustin and me without a word. But when they had passed, the singing began.

"*Swing low, sweet Rustin Parr*
The devil's gonna carry you home . . ."

Parr's expression didn't change the whole time: from when the inmates first raised their voices till the song faded away into the depths of the penitentiary.

I sat there in Rustin's cell, on the cot next to him, and looked again at what the bandage on his arm had been covering. A mass of scar tissue. A riot of ugly colors—black, and blue, and a horrible, sickly green. I suddenly remembered what Charlie Hobart had told me during the trial.

"How did you get this, Rustin?"

No answer.

"Did you do it to yourself?"

"It was the only way, Father. I couldn't let them come through me, the way they did Ranger." Parr held his arm closer then, and pointed to the scars. "Look."

Kyle Brody

For the first time, I thought I saw something underneath the scar tissue and discolored skin; the remnants of a pattern.

"I know my Bible," Parr said. "I knew what I had to do."

He stood and began pacing the cell.

"Isaiah six:six. 'Then flew one of the seraphim unto me, having a live coal in his hand, which he had taken with the tongs from off the altar: and he laid it upon my mouth, and said, Lo, this hath touched thy lips; and thine iniquity is taken away, and thy sin purged.' "

I shook my head. "I don't understand."

"I am cleansed."

My stomach rolled.

"Rustin, you didn't—"

"That's what I wanted to confess to you, Father. I know it wasn't for me to do. To myself, or to the children."

A single tear escaped from the corner of his eye.

"I came back to the house," Parr said. "After Ranger died. Somebody had written all over the walls. I made myself a little hidey-hole in the woods and got comfortable. I knew they'd be coming back."

He continued pacing.

"I couldn't stop it, Father. I couldn't stop it. But at least"—he wiped his nose with the edge of his sleeve—"at least I saved them from the worst. When the killing was done, I went back into the house and dug 'em up. And then I—" he shook his head. "Bless me, Father, for I have sinned."

"Rustin." I stood up. "What are you trying to say? That someone else killed those children?"

He nodded.

"Who did it, Rustin? Who?"

He looked me in the eye then and I knew. I suppose, in the depths of my soul I'd known all along.

What followed is a haze to me.

I am sure I absolved that man, that most innocent of souls, of his sins.

I believe I encouraged him to go to the authorities with his story.

I also remember him telling me he was tired of fighting for his place in the world, tired of living apart and alone for so long. He was looking forward, he said, to being with his parents, his brother, and his dog once again, in God's kingdom.

"The only thing I kind of worry about now, Father," he said, "is you."

Or perhaps he told me that earlier, as I entered his cell.

More and more, I am having trouble keeping everything straight in my head.

What I do remember is the sound of the cell door, clanking shut behind me, and the disgusted look on the guard's face as we walked back toward the warden's office.

"See?" he said. "I told you he was a loon."

The morning of Parr's execution came, a cold bitter day.

I gave Rustin his last rites; a newspaper reporter interviewed me. What I told him exactly, I can't remember.

I stood by Rustin at the end, as he walked up the gallows, and they slipped the hood over his face. I could not watch what came next.

I heard the sound of the lever being pulled, the trapdoor swinging open . . .

And then a cheer went up from the assembled crowd.

It was, without a doubt, the ugliest sound I have ever heard in my life.

I looked over all of them with what I was sure was barely concealed disgust . . .

And my eyes fell on Carol Brody, who stood next to her husband, her arm linked in his. Kyle was on her other side, looking up at his mother.

As I watched, she put her arm around the boy and drew him close.

Then, as if she knew all along I was watching, she raised her gaze to mine, and smiled.

*   *   *

I left Monsignor Fannon a note at the rectory, stating my intentions.

Then I gathered my things together into a duffel and walked to the bus station, where I caught the Greyhound bus first to Philadelphia, and then on to New York City.

Two weeks later the Japanese bombed Pearl Harbor. By the first of the year both Vince and I were in uniform serving God and country.

June 30

Witches, as I have said, were about the devil's business. They tempted with the lure of riches, and power, and the pleasures of the flesh. They used an array of enchantments and magic granted to them by Satan.

Their ultimate goal, of course, the corruption and degradation of all that is good and holy in man.

Our wedding.

Dancing with Mary's ninety-year-old grandmother, who I guess to be all of four and a half feet tall and ninety pounds soaking wet.

"You take care of our little girl. She's special."

"Oh, I will," I promised.

And I did.

Mary and I never, ever argued.

We watched the couples around us whose only way of relating to each other seemed to be sniping and snide remarks and raised voices, and thought ourselves lucky.

We never grew tired of each other.

I woke in the night, to an itching on my arm, and the smell of lilacs.

chapter seventeen

I'm a fast reader. An hour after the package arrived, I was in the reception area at the burn center. So, to my surprise, was Detective Yamana.

"He called you too?" Yamana said, getting up from his seat.

I looked at him and shook my head. "Who?"

"That doctor? He called you too?"

"No. I came because—"

"Detective!"

Yamana and I turned and saw Juarez walking down the hall toward us. "Thanks for coming. This is what I was telling you about."

Juarez handed Yamana a red, letter-size folder with the name *Cazale* on the index tab.

"What is it?" I asked.

Juarez turned to me. "Dominick's medical chart. He'd stopped going to his regular doctor, and was seeing another one, down in Miami. That's why I had such a hard time finding up-to-date records."

Yamana lifted the folder and began flipping through it.

"That also explains why the morphine wasn't working so well: he was on a couple other medications that were interacting with it and lessening its effects." Juarez smiled, and then a frown crossed his face. "Wait a minute—what are you doing here?"

"Cazale sent me this," I said, holding up the journal. "A diary he'd been keeping. I wanted you—"

"This is what you mean, right?" Yamana interrupted. He was studying one page of Cazale's chart intently. "Dementia."

"That's right," Juarez said. "You wanted an explanation for his actions, Detective? There it is."

"I guess so," Yamana said thoughtfully. He licked his index finger and turned a page on the chart. "He's been pretty sick for a long time."

"Sick?" Juarez shook his head. "He's dying."

"Yeah," Yamana said. "What a way to go."

I'd wondered what had prompted Dominick Cazale to break his silence of sixty years. Now I knew; he wanted to make peace with the past.

"A journal, huh? I'm surprised he had the mental wherewithal to write anything down," Juarez said.

"It falls apart at the end," I admitted. "And there are things in there that are a little difficult to swallow."

Yamana held out his hand. "All right, give it here."

He took the journal. I took the folder.

"Confusion on Dominick's part is understandable," Juarez said. "That's the thing about dementia. You mix up pieces of the past: things that happened and didn't happen, things you dreamed about. That's what was going on with Dominick."

I was listening to him and scanning Cazale's chart at the same time. When I came to the biographical notes at the top of the page, I stopped.

Dominick Cazale, born 1915, Baltimore. St. Mary's Hospital.
Siblings: Vincent 1913–1988 (deceased); Joseph, 1917–1940
(deceased).
Married Mary Kathleen Shaughnessy, 1949.
No children.

"Dr. Juarez?" A nurse was standing in the hallway leading to the burn unit.

"Excuse me a second," Juarez said. "I'll be right back." He walked over to consult with her.

Yamana snorted and handed me back the journal. "This is all that witch crap again. And it makes even less sense than that TV show we watched." He eyed me suspiciously. "Tell me the truth. You don't believe any of this stuff—do you?"

I thought about that a moment.

That I, of everyone he knew, might believe what Cazale had written was no doubt why he had sent me the journal. That Dominick had been living in a dream world was undeniable, however: his chart was proof of that.

Joe had died in 1940. Dominick had married the girl he'd dreamed of all those years, Mary Kathleen Shaughnessy. As for the rest of it . . .

The writing on the walls of Rustin Parr's house was certainly real.

As was the copy of the article from the *Washington Post* in my back pocket.

And I'd seen the writing on Cazale's arm . . . hadn't I?

"I notice you didn't answer my question," Yamana said.

"I'm thinking."

He shook his head and wagged a finger at me. "You, my friend, need to get out more often."

Juarez rejoined us then. "It'all is moot at this point."

He took the folder from my hand, a pen from his shirt pocket, and added an entry to the first line on Cazale's chart.

Died July 15, 2000, Broward County General Hospital.

I went back to the hotel and packed.

acknowledgments

For help in understanding what happened to Dominick Cazale in Burkittsville: Ben Rock, Jim Bloom, William Haskins, and Jeff Mills.

For refreshing my knowledge of the historical circumstances surrounding this story:

Argersinger, Joann E. *Toward a New Deal in Baltimore.* Chapel Hill: University of North Carolina Press, 1988.

Carey, George G. *Maryland Folk Legends and Folk Songs.* Cambridge, Maryland: Tidewater Publishers, 1971.

Footner, Hubert. *Maryland Main and the Eastern Shore.* New York and London: D. Appleton-Century Company, 1942.

Greeley, Father Andrew M. *Confessions of a Parish Priest: An Autobiography.* New York: Simon and Schuster, 1986.

Grimassi, Raven. *The Wiccan Mysteries: Ancient Origins and Teachings.* Minnesota: Llewellyn Publications, 1998.

Hill, Douglas and Pat Williams. *The Supernatural.* New York: New American Library, 1967.

Husband, Joseph. *A Year in a Coal-Mine*. Boston and New York: Houghton Mifflin, 1911.

Mitchell, Robert D., ed. *Appalachian Frontiers: Settlement, Society, and Development in the Preindustrial Era*. Lexington: University of Kentucky Press, 1991.

Stuber, Stanley, ed. *The Illustrated Bible and Church Handbook*. New York: Galahad Books, 1966.

Writer's Program. *Maryland: A Guide to the Old Line State*. New York: Oxford University Press, 1940.

www.goth.net/~shanmonster/witch/index.html

www.newadvent.org/cathen

For aid in the transcription of Dominick Cazale's journal, in particular the sections dealing with Rustin Parr, I must cite the collective work of Beinhorn, Cameron, Cornell, O'Brien, Shepherd, and Thayil, in particular 31454-0198-2.

Any errors of interpretation or offensive insensitivities are completely my own.

For more about the author: http://more.at/dastern

I would also like to thank the following:

At Pocket Books: Margaret Clark, Scott Shannon, Judith Curr, Kara Welsh, Donna O'Neill, and Penelope Haynes.

At ICM: Lisa Bankoff and Patrick Price.

At Artisan: Amorette Jones, Ferrell McDonald, and Sonia Imperato.

At Haxan: Dan Myrick, Eduardo Sanchez, Rob Cowie, Mike Monello, and Gregg Hale.

On the other side of Manhattan: Dan Slater.

Down the hill: Dunkin' Donuts.

On the couch: Jill, Cleo, Toni, Madeleine, and . . .